I0780180

PARIS 1984

THE DRIFTER

CAROLIN STAATS-BINDER

AOS Publishing, 2024

Copyright © 2024

Carolin Staats-Binder

All rights reserved under International
and Pan-American copyright conventions

ISBN: 978-1-990496-88-2

Cover Design: Chanelle Poupart

This is a work of fiction. All characters and places are fabricated and
any resemblance to any real persons is unintentional.
Visit AOS Publishing's website:
www.aospublishing.com

TABLE OF CONTENTS

CHAPTER ONE: OVERNIGHT TO PARIS 1

CHAPTER TWO: RUDI 14

CHAPTER THREE: EIFFEL TOWER 24

CHAPTER FOUR: THE BIRD DROPPING 37

CHAPTER FIVE: NOTRE DAME 44

CHAPTER SIX: THE BELL TOWERS..........................51

CHAPTER SEVEN: A SURPRISE VISIT............................58

CHAPTER EIGHT: LE SACRÉ CŒUR.........................71

CHAPTER NIEN: L'ARC DE TRIOMPHE...............87

CHAPTER TEN: LAST DAY IN PARIS 105

CHAPTER ELEVEN: AU BON ACCUEIL 118

CHAPTER TWELVE: CAMP OUT AND DEPARTURE 127

CHAPTER THIRTEEN: RUDI'S VISIT 158

EPILOGUE 179

QUESTIONS FOR READERS AND BOOK CLUBS.........................181

OVERNIGHT TO PARIS

Uncomfortable in my middle seat, I cast a sleepy glance at Aubrey, who was dozing by the window in a row of seats across from me. Taking a closer look at her in that dim compartment, I realized how grossly overweight she was. Her porky figure spilled over the seat. I could hear her snore and see tiny sweat pearls on her forehead.

How did I end up with just this one friend during the last four of my high school years? Why am I travelling with her? Ever since that incident at our graduation last week, which wasn't entirely her fault, I've been wondering whether I can call Aubrey my friend at all.

"Excuse me. May I get to my window seat?" The voice spoke with an urgent, squeaky tone in broken English. I quickly moved my feet out of the way. The owner of the voice had opened the compartment door and was trying not to trip over and step onto feet, small backpacks, and purses. The woman took the last available seat next to me by the window across from Aubrey, who had barely stirred in her sleep with this stop somewhere in Belgium. Passengers were now staying in aisles hunched over open windows. Some had spread out their sleeping bags in the aisles and were getting ready to lie down. My watch showed 02:17 a.m. The aisles were packed. There was no way of slithering out of the compartment to the bathroom. How could this train ride to France be so ridiculously overbooked?

The train had come from Warsaw, a city across the border to the east that I had never been to. It was a hot afternoon in early July in Brunswick when the train rushed into the station with breakneck speed like a bat out of hell. Hard to imagine that was only a few hours ago.

"Where exactly are we?" I turned to the new passenger next to me after she had stowed her luggage and settled in. Puzzled, she looked at me. "*Français?* Do you speak French?" I asked her in my clear high school French. She nodded. "Which Belgian city is this?" I pointed to the compartment floor with my right index finger, hoping to make myself better understood.

"Leuven." She didn't lower the tone of her voice, not bothered to wake anyone. "It's located thirty kilometers east of Brussels. That's where I am going, Brussels, and you?" She gave me a long look. Her hair bounced in shoulder-length, silver-blonde waves. Her hazel eyes looked dull and unreadable. "Are you going to Brussels?" Emphasizing every word in her question, she waited for me to answer.

"Paris..."

"That's quite a distance to go. Are you travelling by yourself?"

"No!" I cast a quick, uncomfortable glance at Aubrey, who was rubbing her eyes while reaching for her backpack. She ignored me and the new passenger as she lifted her backpack onto her lap and zipped it open. After a few seconds of backpack diving, she held in her hands the biggest pepperoni stick I had ever seen. With a quick bite of her teeth, she opened the plastic wrapper, and pushed the pepperoni stick up and out. With relish, she took a first big bite and began to munch noisily. Somewhat nauseated, I turned back to the lady next to me. "I am travelling with her, my friend from high school." My eyes wandered to Aubrey across the compartment so the passenger would know who I referred to. My hope was that the look on my face was not revealing any judgements towards Aubrey. "We just graduated last week, and this is our graduation trip — a couple of days in Paris."

"Paris has much sightseeing to offer. Do you have your trip all planned out?" She sat up in her seat, curious. Again, my eyes darted to Aubrey.

"She did all the planning for our stay and also figured out which Paris Métro to take for our various tours. I, myself, would like to practice my French. I enjoy learning foreign languages. She is good at planning. I am good at communicating." The passenger smiled, leaned back in her seat, and cast a glance out the window. I took it as a sign that our short interaction had come to an end. Aubrey was snoozing again.

Brussels came and went. The lady next to me got up, gathered her few belongings, and mumbled a quiet goodbye. She disappeared out the compartment door and was instantly swallowed up in the aisle by many leaving passengers. I took a deep breath and stretched.

"Aubrey, I am heading to the lavatory." Aubrey nodded, giving me an absentminded look. It was obvious she didn't feel all that secure out by herself with a friend, away from her family. The expert scientist at school appeared to be lacking some type of street smart, which left her vulnerable, even when her friend left her side for only a few minutes. I had reached the bathroom at the end of the train wagon. "Oh my!" I took a good look at my face in the tiny mirror while searching for my hairbrush in my pocket. My face was glistening with moisture that had collected between my skin and my make-up. There was nothing left of the foundation other than blotches that gave my face the appearance of a dot-to-dot board game. "Can't wait to get to Paris, have some breakfast in a Parisian café, and then take the Métro to our booked youth hostel. I need to freshen up in a hot shower," I mumbled to my sleepy-looking face in the mirror and began to smile thinking about our upcoming adventures. At least I was not travelling alone, if only with a classmate who might not be fun to have around, and by the looks of it, might become somewhat of a burden. Little did I know I wouldn't be taking a shower any time soon.

***

The hot, stuffy air in Paris engulfed us. The exhaust around the train station made it impossible to breathe some fresh air. It was an almost cloudless day with the relentless heat of the July sun above us. I blinked at the sudden brightness.

"Hey, Aubrey, look over there; a café called 'Le Petit Déjeuner'. Let's go for breakfast." I smiled.

"What does *déjeuner* mean again?" She sounded insecure and gave me a puzzled look.

"Breakfast. Don't you remember anything from our French lessons with that old spinster Miss...?" I regretted my question in an instant, knowing that she wouldn't remember after opting out of French as soon as she could.

"I am not as talented in languages as you are. So don't judge me if I cannot remember. You are the one who will get us by for the next few days. Let's check out 'Le Petit

Déjeuner'." In silence, we crossed the street. "By the way, I want to call home!"

"Of course you do. We'll find a phone booth after breakfast."

"There's one over there."

"Later!"

All kinds of sweet and savoury croissants were looking at us. "*Café, s'il vous plaît,*" I addressed the waiter. "*Deux au lait,*" I added.

"What is '*deux au lait*'," Aubrey wanted to know while scanning my facial expression from the side. I gave her a quick incredulous look.

"Two cups of coffee with milk!" I said impatiently, turning away to face the waiter again, who was busy preparing our order behind the counter. Without looking at Aubrey, I said to her, "I don't feel like croissants. But that's all there is. Which ones will you have?"

The waiter put two small cups in front of us, with more force and noise than necessary. Some of the ochre liquid spilled out of the cups onto the sticky counter. I stared at the tiny cup of 'coffee' in front of me when Aubrey burst out in French, "*Un croissant au jambon, s'il vous plaît.* See, I do remember some of my French," she sounded self-important and then cast me a challenging look from her bar-stool beside me. I ignored her by addressing the waiter.

"*Monsieur, c'est du café, ça?* Is this American coffee?"

"Espresso," he answered, wiping down the counter. "*Pas de café américain*; no American coffee here." He disappeared behind a door for employees only.

"No coffee," I mumbled in disbelief.

"Are you not eating anything?" Aubrey asked. She waited, watching me taste the strong espresso.

"No. I still have a snack. I'll eat at the youth hostel. Hopefully, they'll have *un goûter* before dinner. I can't drink this dark espresso. It is too strong for my taste." I pushed my half-finished cup down the counter. "No rush, Aubrey. Take your time. I will make my way to the ladies' room."

"What's '*un goûter*'?"

"A Snack!"

"Ahhh," Aubrey exclaimed, taking a sip of the extra strong stuff. "Not bad, not bad!" She said it loud enough for me to hear down the hallway to the washroom. I turned around and saw her take a cautious bite of her ham and cheese croissant. She looked content for the time being, enjoying her *petit déjeuner.*

I opened the washroom door and stopped in my tracks, incredulous. *Is this... This is... A toilet... Hah... I remember a friend telling me that French toilets may look different. It's a shower tub rather than the bowl we're used to. So I'll have to squat. How's a person going to get comfortable using that shower tub version of a toilet for urgent physiological needs? And it stinks, too. This grubby place was definitely not a good choice for* le petit déjeuner.

***

Aubrey led the way to the closest Paris Métro that would take us to the *arrondissement* of our youth hostel. For the time being, she had forgotten that she wanted to phone her parents.

"Kudos to you, Aubrey. I would never find my way around this maze. How do you know which direction we have to take?" She pointed to the unfolded map in her hands.

"It's all on here. You just have to read it." A rumbling noise from a distance had us perk up. Here was our first ever Métro ride, slowing down for us and for many others. The noise gradually faded to a puff. Finally the Métro stopped. The doors flew open and out came flowing the longest stream of Parisians, mingling with the waiting crowd on an already overcrowded platform. We had to make a run for it to get in before the doors closed. The Métro started slow at first and then picked up speed as we hurried into tunnels of darkness and back out of them into daylight, only to be swallowed up again underground all the way to the next stop.

"Feels like a rollercoaster ride," I said, feeling queasy to my stomach. "How much longer?"

"Four more stops," Aubrey answered, shifting her weight from one foot to the other while holding on to seat backs. We hadn't managed to find empty seats and remained standing in the aisle stuck back to back to others. The guy standing behind me smelled like an overdose of Gauloises tobacco. Little did I know this wouldn't be my last encounter with Gauloises. I buried my nose in my sleeve. *I need to get off.*

Our stop came. Pushing ahead to the doors, we jumped off. We hurried out of the Métro station closest to our youth hostel in the sunny mid-afternoon. We both took a breather at the same time, smiling a faint sigh of relief. The fresh air felt so good.

"Down this way," Aubrey pointed west. I realized how tomato-red and sweaty her face looked in the heat. Her breathing was heavy. Her feet wanted to give way under the weight of her heavy backpack. In fact, her feet looked tiny as they carried her obesity.

"We can take a break," I suggested, feeling empathetic towards her for her over-exertion to keep up with my pace. She didn't argue.

"Okay. There's a bench over there." I didn't mean to sit down, but we headed for the bench anyway.

"Do you have any water left?" Aubrey looked desperate.

"I may. Let me have a look." I did some backpack diving and handed her my last unopened bottle of water. She took it eagerly and gulped down the water in the blink of an eye, not worried about spilling some on her outfit.

"Water has never tasted better!" Aubrey exclaimed. She laughed, tossed her backpack onto the bench, and hopped onto the grass to lie down. Her breathing slowed as she took a peek at the afternoon sun. I stood there in front of the bench watching her with anticipation. I hadn't taken my pack off my shoulders as a sure sign I was anxious to get to our accommodation. Tired, hungry, and in need of a shower, I longed for a place to relax, a room that offered protection from a busy, crowded metropolitan like Paris.

"Look at the Eiffel Tower in the distance." I pointed with my sunglasses dangling off my index finger. "It looks unique. This whole city has unique historical monuments, and I can't wait to see them. Shall we go?"

***

I could see the immense terrain of the youth hostel from a distance. Tents of all shapes, sizes, and colours were set up all over the lawn.

"Finally!" I uttered with relief as we approached the entrance with a quicker step. The large glass doors led into a hall. I welcomed the fresh, cool air upon entering. Aubrey and I headed straight towards the reception, a huge front desk with several agents attending to tourists. Here was my chance to practice my French. We needed to get the keys to our room. "*Notre chambre pour deux, s'il vous plaît. Our room for two, please.*"

"*Votre nom, s'il vous plaît?*"

"*Je m'appelle Carielle.*" I directed my attention to Aubrey. "*Mon amie s'appelle Aubrey.* In April, I booked a room for us, or let's say two beds in a dormitory. We just got off the train from Germany this morning."

"*Oui, oui, votre nom de famille, s'il vous plaît!*" The front desk agent began to sound somewhat impatient while answering the phone and taking notes, making us no big priority.

"Carielle Sander." I sounded deflated and glanced helplessly at Aubrey. The agent began to look through paperwork in her drawers below the counter, ignoring us.

"Do you have confirmation for your reservation? I am unable to find your name for today's check-in. "At last, she looked up at me with a sourly bored expression as I pulled out of my purse an orange piece of thick paper the size of an index card. It had the word 'vouchers' written in pen at the top of it. The agent took it out of my hand without delay and briefly scanned it. Handing it back to me, she shook her head. "You don't have a reservation with us. You were to send vouchers to hold a reservation. We never received vouchers from you. Do you have a tent?" I looked at her incredulously.

"A tent? Of course not!" I took another helpless look at Aubrey, who shifted from one foot to the other, clearly wondering what was going on. Her eyes kept darting from me to the agent and back to me, and back to the agent. Aubrey didn't appear to understand.

"I am sorry I cannot help you. We have no empty beds at this time of the year," the agent concluded, apparently at the end with our interaction.

"Where can we stay?" I stammered in disbelief.

"There's just about no vacancy in Paris in July. Next, please." She turned to the next guest in line behind us and left us standing there at a loss of words and further action.

"I thought you said you had looked after our reservation, and that everything was booked and ready to go," Aubrey snapped at me. While she had a point, I couldn't handle her throwing that accusation at me. She was right, but I wasn't going to admit it, so I said nothing in return.

Undecided, I stood around in silence, absorbed in a spiral of thoughts about our options. Reluctantly, I turned around and took another glance back at the reception, where the agent was now helping three new guests, one girl, two guys, all with heavy knapsacks on their backs and hiking boots on their feet. They appeared to be older than us, and one of them spoke to the agent in broken English. The agent appeared to have forgotten about us. She took no longer notice of our presence, though we had not resolved to leave. Was I hoping for a turn of events? A miracle? Two beds magically appearing? Dragging our feet, we made our way back to the entrance. Exhausted, Aubrey faced me.

"What are we going to do? Go home?" Her voice sounded shrill.

"That would be an option, but we just arrived. I would like to see the Eiffel Tower. We could stay until tonight, and then take the overnight train back to Germany."

"How could this happen? I spent days trying to figure out what to pack. I paid for the train ride, only to go home again on the day we arrived. What a waste of time and money! You were in charge of the reservation!" Aubrey stared at me furiously. I took a step back. In fact, I had never seen her so angry and loud. She couldn't keep her voice down. Her face was dotted with sweat pearls as it had been since the previous night on the train. Her hair stood on end as if she had just crawled out of bed.

"I know it's my fault. I'll make it up to you." I sounded defeated. "I clearly didn't understand the voucher thing. I thought we were all set."

RUDI

"Hello there. Anything wrong? You girls look upset. Can I help?" The guy who had been talking to a fellow down the hall approached us straight on. I didn't see it coming, and surprisingly, he addressed us in German. I had noticed him earlier in focused conversation, and never thought we would attract his attention. He had appeared very absorbed in his interaction with the other man, who was now nowhere to be seen. Strangely enough, though, I instantly felt relieved to meet a person who appeared to be a native German speaker. I also had instant confidence in him without being able to explain why. Maybe it was because he was German. Maybe it was because Aubrey and I had no solution to our dilemma and had reached some kind of a dead end. Maybe the guy would offer a way out.

He stood there looking from Aubrey to me, and then he rested his eyes on my face. He smiled. "What's happening?" At first glance, I saw his wavy dark blond hair, his brown eyes, and a missing tooth. Aubrey shrugged and stayed silent. It appeared she wanted to leave the response up to me, which could've been to keep his nose out of it, but a response like that never crossed my mind. The guy looked amused about us being caught off-guard. He had offered his help, and we were uncertain about how to respond to him.

"We have no place to stay. I thought I had booked a reservation with this youth hostel but I never sent the vouchers they had asked for." It felt good to let it all out.

"When did you get to Paris?"

"Just this morning on the overnight train from Brunswick. Looks like we might be headed back to Germany tonight."

"No need to rush home just yet. I know of a place where you can stay. I can take you there. I am going that direction, anyway. It's a short Métro ride from here." The guy sounded serious. Aubrey took a step back as if unsure whether to accept help from a complete stranger.

"I don't know…" Aubrey said quietly. Her anger appeared to have vanished into thin air. She seemed shy and insecure.

"How much a night would it cost?" I was curious about this unexpected chance of a possible overnight stay in Paris.

"I can't say for sure, but it wouldn't be more than the youth hostel. It's a very simple accommodation but it would give you a chance to stay in Paris for your vacation. How long of a stay, you said?"

"Just a few days," I responded eagerly. "Aubrey, shall we take a look?" Aubrey looked sweaty, panicky, and hesitant.

"I would like to call my family," she answered. The guy briefly scanned Aubrey, said nothing, and turned to me with the same amused look on his face. He shrugged.

"It doesn't hurt to go see it. What other options do we have besides returning home?" I was hoping I made some sense. Aubrey nodded briefly and picked up her backpack. It felt like she didn't have much physical energy left in her for this unexpected undertaking. I didn't want her to collapse, but I definitely wanted to check out this option.

"Let's go," the guy said. He glanced at my bags. "Let me carry your small case. That's a lot of stuff you girls are lugging around for a couple of days." He laughed. It was an unfamiliar sound. "Have you had anything to eat?"

"Just what we have for snacks. I didn't eat anything at the café this morning. Aubrey did. I can wait. I would like to get settled first." He laughed again, not offering his help to Aubrey, who had strapped her pack on her back by then. She carried her other two items. He walked beside me all the way to the Métro station. New to Paris, I didn't have a clue where we were or where we were going. Nonetheless, I had no doubts about his good intentions.

"So what's your name, by the way?"

"I am Rudi. What's yours?"

"I am Carielle, and this is Aubrey, as you already know. Have you been in Paris long? Do you live here?"

"Yes."

"How long?" I was all ears.

"Long enough…" He looked the other way, signalling that there would be no extension to the answer. I decided not to poke for more. We reached the Métro station. Rudi moved along in a familiar way. He had probably walked all of Paris many times. It was home. *Home? Where would he be living?* Why did it cross my mind that he might not have a home? I took a closer, furtive look at his appearance. His jeans were worn and baggy. His shirt was one of the old-fashioned types, beige with a pattern and mundane; maybe like the ones my dad would wear occasionally, but less fancy.

My contemplation about Rudi had ended when I found myself on another underground platform of the Parisian Métro. I welcomed the cooler temperature despite the trapped humidity. People walked by in a hurry dressed to the nines, giving off a scent of strong perfume or aftershave. And Aubrey… She had finally caught up. She had been trailing a few meters behind us in complete silence. She looked pale and worried. Cold sweat was running down her face.

"I haven't called home yet," she said, short of breath.

"You will once we get to our accommodation." I quickly followed Rudi onto the Métro to an empty bench. He occupied it with the speed of lightning before anyone could get ahead of him. He sat down by the window and motioned me to sit beside him, which would've left Aubrey standing next to us. I knew Aubrey was at her wit's end and offered her my seat instead. "I don't mind standing." Aubrey looked at me with an air of gratefulness and sat down. She moved as closely to the edge of the bench as possible, away from Rudi. Off we went as before, up into the daylight and back down into the darkness. The Métro ride took thirty-five minutes, and this time not even Aubrey knew where we were going.

***

We ended up standing in front of a tall stone house, a row house. It spelled medieval times and historic events. I took a look around and realized the whole area was designed that way.

"Just wait here. I will go in and talk to reception." Rudi's voice left no choice in the matter despite his gentle tone of a caring nature. Backpacks now sitting at our feet, Aubrey and I waited patiently on the sidewalk outside the door. The day was waning. I really needed to eat. Aubrey studied her map.

"Is there a restaurant or grocery store nearby?" I wanted to know.

"Just wait," Aubrey snapped. "I am making a lame attempt at finding out where in this hellish city we are."

"Hellish? That's a good way of putting it!" I sounded sarcastic without wanting to. Maybe the long trip was putting us over the edge.

"Carielle, I don't want to be here. I don't like this. We don't know this guy. Who knows what kind of a dump this accommodation is that he's trying to put us up in. We're not even in there with him to hear what they're arranging for us. What if..." She fell silent at the sound of the door opening.

"All set!" Rudi appeared on the doorstep with a smile. "Come here and listen." Aubrey and I moved closer to him. "They have a room with two single beds and a sink. The toilets are down the hall. If you want to shower, you'll have to go all the way downstairs, to the cellar." Aubrey and I exchanged a quick glance. She rolled her eyes. I tried hard to keep my expression as neutral as possible. I really wanted this to work out for us.

"Okay," I responded, a little too cheerful. "How much?"

"Sixty francs a night. Sounds good?" His question didn't leave room for a negative response.

"Yes, that sounds reasonable. What do you think, Aubrey?" I wanted Rudi to realize that it wasn't just my opinion that mattered. He had been acting as though Aubrey didn't exist. We now both stared at Aubrey. She shrugged, turned sideways, and took another good look at the building. Rudi and I waited patiently, following her gaze.

"Fine!" She barked.

"Well, that settles it. I'll be on my way." Rudi turned to leave as Aubrey was getting ready to approach the entrance, backpack in tow. I stood bewildered.

"Rudi, you are leaving? Just like that? We haven't even had a chance to thank you for your help."

"Don't you worry about it. Oh, by the way, this hotel is run by Moroccans. I've known the owners of this hotel for a long time. I've made sure that you will be safe in their care." Rudi took a long look at me. His sudden departure was dragging out. I didn't know what to say but then asked the essential question.

"How can we get in touch with you?"

"Tell the young guy at the reception. He will contact me on your part. I can be here in a flash if needed. Now enjoy your stay." He gave a wave with his right hand at shoulder height to signal his exit was for real now.

"Bye," I whispered almost inaudibly and watched as he skipped away as mysteriously as he had appeared, out of nowhere into nowhere. Little did I know that this feature of his would be following me until the end.

***

I had so many questions for him. *Where do you live in this megalopolis? Where do you work? Do you have a family?* Nothing but questions popped into my head after he was out of sight and out of reach. A family? Did he look like a family man?

"We may never see him again," I said more to myself than to Aubrey as I picked my luggage off the sidewalk by my feet.

"What?" Aubrey appeared to have misunderstood or just played dumb.

"Do you mean to say you want to see this drifter again?" She challenged me. I just sent her a serious look across the sidewalk and remained silent. I had no interest in starting an argument about Rudi at this stage of our long day, and I had to share a room with her on top of it, starting in a moment. Aubrey went ahead and finally opened the heavy wooden door. It creaked as if to announce a gruesome entry. Single file, we stepped into the dark hallway.

We walked a few steps, dragging our bags with our last bit of physical strength, and came across the reception — a counter — to the right. A very young guy, extremely handsome, greeted us courteously.

"*Bonjour Mesdemoiselles!*" *How old would the receptionist be? Sixteen? I am nineteen.* Dark complexion, oval face, dark brown eyes and hair. *Even more attractive when he speaks French...* An older gentleman was sitting off to the right behind him, watching the whole scene like a hawk. *Hotel manager, guardian, or dad...* He appeared at ease with the situation.

"*Voici la clé. Vous pouvez payer plus tard.*" The youth pushed the key across the counter to me. Aubrey stood off to the side as if she was no participant in this game for two travellers. I didn't need to explain anything to the young receptionist. Rudi had already taken care of the details. Aubrey still stood there, staring at him, hesitant. I quickly translated for her.

"He said we can pay later." She nodded. I took the key to room 103, first floor.

"*Des questions, Mademoiselle?*"

"*Est-ce qu'il y a un restaurant près d'ici?*"

"Free Time, like McDonald's, just one block over to the left. They're open until eleven."

"Good to know. Thank you." I smiled politely at the youngster and then at the older gentleman in the background before turning to Aubrey with the key in my hands. "Let's go." I gave her a sign to follow me.

There was no elevator in the old building. We had to take the steep steps up.

"I may have to go up and down multiple times to get all my bags up to the room," Aubrey groaned.

"Just take what you can. I'll come right back down to get what's left." I was halfway up the stairs when the handsome young guy appeared at the bottom of the stairs, grabbed our remaining luggage, and took it up to our room for us. He left it outside the door and turned to leave.

"That's very nice of you. *Merci beaucoup!*" I felt I was the one of us still remembering my manners at the end of this intriguing day. Aubrey said nothing.

"Let's dump the luggage and go to Free Time for dinner before it gets dark. I haven't eaten, as you know. I am mostly looking forward to a hot cup of green tea." For the first time in hours, I felt a sense of relief, while Aubrey had turned completely introverted.

THREE

EIFFEL TOWER

"Eiffel Tower today?" I asked Aubrey, who was just stepping into her dark blue corduroy pants from a day of extended travelling.

"Yes. I've already figured out how to get to Le Champs de Mars in the seventh *arrondissement*."

"Is that where the Eiffel Tower is located?"

"Sure thing. As you can see, I did my homework — my prep work, so to speak." By the sounds of it, she was challenging me again about the flop with the youth hostel.

"Yes, I can see that. You obviously want to say that I failed to do mine. I apologized for it. I know you are not comfortable here."

"Of course I am not comfortable here. Look at this door! The wood is brittle. The lock barely keeps us safe here. It could theoretically be opened in seconds from the outside.

Simply put, some of those gentlemen here would have to put in very little effort to kick the door in. And you know it."

"No one will."

"How can you be so sure? Just because you trust the drifter?"

"End of topic! Let's get back to the Eiffel Tower. Are you ready to go?"

"Almost! Where will we have breakfast?"

"Free Time again! That's all we can afford. They have apple turnovers. I can't wait to have one."

"By the way, the French call the Eiffel Tower *'La Dame de Fer'* — The Iron Lady. They started constructing it in 1887, and it was finished in 1889. The Eiffel Tower was the World's Fair centerpiece of 1889." Aubrey studied the map that had a section of things you may want to know to the side of it.

"Interesting. The French must've been proud of Gustave Eiffel's conception. After all, there's no such unique-looking tower anywhere else in the world."

"Not necessarily. Some French artists and intellectuals criticized the design."

"As I meant to say, unique by any standards! Do you have your gear for the day?"

"I am ready."

"So am I. Let's lock up and get out of here. Will you find the way back to the hotel this afternoon?"

"Of course! Why are you asking?"

"You are right. I should know better than to question you."

***

I stood in awe on Le Champs de Mars, a few metres away from the Eiffel Tower, admiring the wrought-iron lattice structure of a tourist attraction in the capital of France. Slim and elegant, it reached into the sky. Like so many parks in Paris, Le Champs de Mars was well-kept with perfectly pruned trees and shrubs, neatly arranged flower beds, and a healthy-looking lawn — an open invitation for sunbathers and picnickers. I sank into the grass and took a good look at my surroundings. The grass felt soft like moss. Aubrey stood close to me with her nose in her map.

"The Eiffel Tower has been 'un monument historique' since 1964," she read self-importantly.

"Can we walk up?" I squinted in the sunlight, taking it all in.

"The Tower has three levels. We can walk as far up as the second level. It says here it has restaurants on the first and second levels."

"Probably unaffordable," I cautioned matter-of-factly. "Let's go. I would like to climb the stairs to the second level. Would there be a fee for walking up?"

"I am not sure. We'll find out when we get there. I imagine we'll need tickets — regardless — if we want to take the lift to the third level." We slowly approached the Eiffel Tower. It was surrounded by tourists with languages from all corners of the world, most of whom I didn't understand.

"Aubrey, this is impressive." I scanned the Eiffel Tower in all its detail. "Can we really not climb all the way to the top?" Without answering my question, she went to stand in line at the ticket counter. "I'll wait here," I called over to her. She nodded from a distance and rearranged her sun hat. *Those corduroy pants on her must be too hot and uncomfortable.* I directed my attention towards the top of the Eiffel Tower and was able to see it. The lift was moving upwards at a snail's speed, like a mouse inside a snake body, just in the opposite direction; not down, but up. In a while, Aubrey was back. She handed me a ticket.

"It's free to climb all the way up to the second level. I purchased tickets for the lift from the second to the third level."

"Fantastic! Look up, Aubrey, I've been watching the lift. Isn't it genius?" She ignored my observation.

"Just so you are aware... It's over three hundred steps to the first level and another three hundred steps from the first level to the second level."

"So there's no choice but to ride up to the third level?"

"Carielle, I told you... No! There is a staircase to the top but it's not accessible to tourists."

"How tall is the Tower?" I was curious. Out came Aubrey's map again.

"It's three hundred and thirty metres tall." With anticipation, we had reached the first step to the first level. Excited, I stepped onto it.

"Wow! You can see right through the stairs to the ground. Breathtaking! This may not be convenient for those who are afraid of heights. What about you, Aubrey?"

"I'll manage if we go slow." I was five steps up and moving along by the time Aubrey had set her foot on the second stair. Standing right inside the Eiffel Tower, I enjoyed the view up through the wrought-iron lattice towards the lift and the way down towards the ground with its teeming of people from around the world. Breathless, I stopped on the first level, which was almost completely taken up by the restaurant. I didn't bother checking the menu and waited for Aubrey to catch up. Rosy-cheeked and sweaty, she finally caught up.

"I am afraid of heights," she exclaimed.

"Will you be able to go on?" Excited for the climb to the second level, I was only half-heartedly interested in her response. I had already moved away from her towards the next set of stairs when she called over to me.

"No choice since I bought myself a ticket to go all the way up. I'll be okay."

"Sounds good. See you up there." I scampered away. In no time I had reached the second level. The platform was much smaller than Level One's. The restaurant was a cafeteria type of lunch counter. Then I ran into the entrance to the lift. The lift appeared oversized for the shaft it travelled through. I began to feel a bit uneasy. I looked around me.

"Where is Aubrey?" I whispered to myself joining the line-up to the lift. I decided to let people go ahead of me, still waiting for Aubrey. She finally arrived after another ten minutes.

"Sorry, I had to take a few breaks on the way up and drink some water. Is this the line-up to the top?"

"Yes, we may not be on the next lift. More time for us to get used to the idea of traveling up the slim shaft to the top."

"Will be a breathtaking view. I don't mind as long as I don't have to climb any more," Aubrey ended with a smile on her face.

On the way up, there was nothing between the elevator and the view of Paris other than the wrought-iron lattice. I felt almost suspended in the air. The elevator was moving along slowly. What would we encounter at the height of the tip?

"Do you think there will be a lot of people up there?" I murmured to Aubrey.

"Only as many as can fit. They'll drop us off, and take a bunch down."

The elevator came to an abrupt stop; the door opened. With more anticipation, we got off the lift. It was breezy. We walked around the top platform in circles a number of times to get some good shots of the Parisian panorama. Despite the summer temperatures, I felt chilly in the breeze. Aubrey and I stood beside each other in silence. Separately, we took it all in, absorbed in our own thoughts.

***

"It was a successful first day in Paris," I said at Free Time where we savoured chicken burgers and chips after a long day of being on our feet. "What's the plan for tomorrow?"

"I'd say Notre Dame," Aubrey suggested, dipping her fries into ketchup. She appeared to really enjoy this fast food dinner.

"Did the flowers last long?" I asked.

"Which flowers?" Aubrey looked perplexed and stopped munching for a moment.

"The flowers my mother gave you for our graduation..." An awkward silence followed my suggestion.

"I think they were still there when we left for Paris. My mom said she would look after them." Aubrey appeared to want to say more but left it at that. The flowers given to her by my mother were obviously not a big deal. Contemplative, I decided to drop the subject for the day. I scanned the restaurant. It was a big bright white room flooded with sunlight. We were the only ones around on the second floor.

"I'd like to take a shower, but I am not comfortable going to the basement by myself with my shower kit. I haven't seen a single female in our hotel accommodation." I looked at Aubrey who shifted uneasily in her chair.

"Neither have I. Why are you concerned? You said the hotel would be fine." Aubrey waited for me to respond.

"It was either that, or going home." I concluded.

***

"*Venez ici.* Come this way!" Alexandre, the young guy from the reception, motioned with his index finger from the dark end of the hallway. I froze in front of the hotel reception, turning my head to cast an insecure glance at Aubrey, who stood behind me, petrified. "*Venez ici. Je vais vous montrer notre salle de télévision.* Our TV room." Standing by a door straight down the hallway, Alexandre waited for us to approach. He had a faint smile on his handsome face. I took a few steps towards him and the door. He opened it. One step behind me, Aubrey followed, smelling of greasy burger and sweat-soaked clothes. *I hope she'll wash up tonight even if it's just at the sink in our room.* I was now close enough to be able to take a good look at the TV room. There were men of Moroccan or Arab descent seated around the room, all staring at a big-screen TV. At the sight of me in the doorframe, they turned around — one by one — and greeted me with a courteous *bonjour.* Some smiled, blowing cigarette smoke into the air. Only Gauloises could smell that way... My eyes began to water.

Aubrey wasn't visible to them yet. She was hiding behind my back. I nodded to Alexandre but said nothing. I was uncomfortable. Seven Moroccans plus Alexandre, plus his dad or whoever he was... I took a deep breath.

"*Venez vous asseoir, Mademoiselle.*" One of them spoke to me. He put out a chair for me to sit down beside him. I didn't move. *Maybe I should accept their courteous invitation, even though I don't want to be here and I don't want to speak with them.* Now Aubrey's face appeared above my left shoulder. The men kept staring at us, and now Aubrey was the focus of their attention.

"Shall we...?" I asked Aubrey under my breath. She was as pale as a starched white linen sheet.

I silently moved across the room like a stalking leopard as if not making any noise with my feet could avert their attention. I sat down just as silently, all seven pairs of eyes on me. Aubrey had not been offered a chair and stopped in her tracks in the middle of nowhere. One of the Moroccans stood up to fetch another chair and placed it next to him across the room from where I was seated. Aubrey sat down clumsily without looking at anyone. The TV room was dead silent for a split second as the volume was turned down with the commercials coming on. Then, from one second to another, they all bombarded me with questions at the same time. I didn't understand a thing. Aubrey appeared to want to disappear in her chair by drooping like a marionette and staring at her hands. I knew that any assistance from her was too much to hope for. I had a hard time understanding their French with an Arabic accent. I heard myself airing fragments of sentences.

"Yes, we are here for a few days. No, I am not from France. No, I am not married. We are on a trip. No, I have never been to France. I am from northern Germany."

They pointed at my lips. I instinctively touched my face.

"Beautiful lips," I heard them say in unison. "No red colour. No red lip colour! Is ugly. French women wear red lips. Ugly! You don't! Beautiful lips. No red!" One of the guys used his right hand to make a swiping motion from left to right in front of his mouth. I guessed it meant lipstick had better be off. Insecure and with fluttering eyelids, I attempted a smile and felt my cheeks blushing. I smiled at a distant corner of the room and was tempted to sink into my absentmindedness, but did not dare lose my alertness around these men.

"You can watch TV with us in the evenings. Any time! Just come down." I nodded to their eager invitation. The fact was I rarely watched TV at home, never mind on vacation. It bored me. There was always something better to do than sitting in front of the tube, like reading an adventure novel, or taking a nap, or going for a walk. Sitting on pins and needles, I wanted to get up and take leave. But I felt glued to the chair. Aubrey didn't seem to exist any longer. Despite her being a big girl, she had faded into nothingness. She would have been trying to be invisible throughout this scenario. Had she called her parents? I couldn't remember. Once out of here, I would never hear the end of it... The hotel, the Moroccans, the drifter. Blame it all on the drifter whom she wished we had never met.

"Do you know Rudi?" I heard myself saying into the crowd. With a furious expression on her face, Aubrey shot me a poisoned look. I ignored her and looked from face to face. However, I didn't catch any signs denoting they might be alarmed. Was I expecting them to know him? Barely noticeable, they shook their heads at the same time.

"Who?" One of them asked. The question darted across the room and hung in midair.

"Rudi used to be a guest in this hotel," Alexandre disclosed from the doorway. All heads turned and stayed on Alexandre's handsome face that revealed nothing other than his neutral statement. Had he been standing there all along?

"Well, gentlemen, it has been a pleasure." I tried my best upper-class behaviour. "It's time for us ladies to retreat. We've had a busy day, and we'll have another busy day ahead of us. It was very nice meeting you all. *Merci de nous avoir invitées à rejoindre votre cercle.* Thank you for inviting us to join your circle." Hastily, I stood up, clutching my backpack with all important documents and all my francs for the holidays. Aubrey got off her seat so quickly she tipped over the chair. It landed on the floor with a loud thud. The Moroccans turned to look at her, clearly unimpressed with her awkwardness. Aubrey blushed and rushed out of the room before me. I saw that she didn't stop to wait for me to catch up with her in the hallway. In a flash, she raced up the stairs to our room. I nodded a friendly *au revoir* to all of them and took my time to leave the room. I didn't want to appear apprehensive. Once on the stairs, I breathed a sigh of relief.

When I reached our room, the door was locked.

"Aubrey, it's me. Open up!" I knocked. I waited. I knocked again. Finally, I heard some heavy footsteps. She unlocked the door in slow motion. I quickly entered, turned around, and relocked the door. Was I going to say anything about the event with the Moroccans, or wait until she'd bring it up, or pretend it never happened?

"We could go on a boat ride on the Seine tomorrow before visiting Notre Dame. The boat rental is within walking distance from Notre Dame," she said matter-of-factly. Against my expectations, Aubrey appeared calm and collected. I hesitated while switching gears to the next day's travel plans.

"Sounds fine. Let's do it." I managed a smile.

"Sorry about locking the door on you. I thought you would stay longer — with the Moroccans I mean."

"Stay longer? I had clearly taken leave when you and I both made our way to the door — separately. You were ahead of me." I was mystified at Aubrey's remark.

"Yeah, but you know what it's like. Sometimes we get sidetracked. We get pulled into another conversation of some sort, and right at the point of leaving." She rolled onto the bed and pulled the covers out from under her weight to tuck herself in.

"That may be with the right company and no language barrier. I was just as relieved to get out of there as you were."

"It didn't look like it. Good night!"

"To bed already?" I stared at the mount of Aubrey's self and her bed sheets, blankets, and pillows. She didn't respond. In a matter of minutes, there was only the sound of her quietly snoring the Parisian sundown away.

THE BIRD DROPPING

"Hey, Aubrey, I found an interesting fact about the river Seine in the side notes of your map."

"What is it?" Showing few signs of interest in my observation, Aubrey scanned the river towards Notre Dame and then spotted the next boat: the one we would take. It looked small, packed with tourists. "It'll be really crammed on the boat. Look at this line-up! You were saying?"

"The Seine is seven hundred and seventy-seven kilometers long." A triple seven in nature didn't sound like a coincidence to me.

"And?" Aubrey demanded. She appeared in a bad mood. She either didn't want to talk or didn't want to understand. I decided to enlighten her, anyway.

"Seven hundred and seventy-seven is a highly spiritual number, a sign of divine guidance." Aubrey didn't comment. She kept staring at the boat. It dawned on me again that she had been neglecting her grooming standards since we had arrived in Paris. She brushed her teeth in the mornings. Unlike me, she didn't use the sink in our room for good hair or body washing. Her hair stood on end in curls. I was beginning to feel embarrassed in her sweaty presence, which my nose failed to ignore.

"I still haven't called home." She kept her focus on the boat with a daydreamer's glare.

"Maybe you could use the phone at the reception for a charge. Why don't you ask Alexandre when we get back to the hotel?" I wanted to cheer her up. Aubrey squinted.

"I don't speak French!" She barked at me and pulled her sunhat farther down into her blotchy face. The heat visibly made her excursions a challenge.

"Next!" The tour guide sounded with a booming voice. It was our turn to board the boat. "*Allez-y, allez-y, allez-y!*" An impatient tour guide didn't make the embarking an easy task for us. He probably saw hundreds of tourists every day and had lost his patience with hesitant travellers. I didn't want to tip sideways and took my time stepping onto the boat and sitting down, despite his shortness with everyone present. I held out my left hand from my boat bench to Aubrey, which she took with an air of gratitude. She slowly sat down across from me, then stared into the distance.

"I can ask Alexandre for you. In French." I offered cautiously.

We didn't say a word to each other during the entire boat tour. Shallow waves splashing against the side of the boat put me into a meditative state. The sun was scorching hot in a cloudless sky. For once, Paris seemed to stand still, with faint traffic noise in the distance. It was Sunday. Notre Dame and other tourist attractions came into view; Notre Dame was a magnificent cathedral with much history like no other. I couldn't wait to immerse myself in its energy while being mindful of its historical value. Soon we would be there...

I turned to Aubrey and froze. My mouth opened on its own accord at the sight of a big blob in her hair. What on Earth...? I took another investigative look, then failed to believe my eyes. A huge bird dropping had landed in her hair above her right eye. The blob was black with a generous white ring around it. My mouth closed and opened again. I didn't know how to get it across to her.

"Aubrey, you know... There's..." I didn't finish. She looked at me as if I was misgiving of my good intentions towards her. I chose to ignore her hostility. Instead, I wordlessly kept staring at the moist blob in her hair. My surprise was so intense, I just about missed the tour guide anchoring the boat and — with utmost impatience — commanding us to disembark. All wobbly on my feet, I stood and climbed out of the boat in two big strides.

Aubrey was the last one to get up. I stood on the shore, helpless and somewhat disgusted. How could she not notice... that feeling?

"Why are you staring at me? You've been staring at me for the past ten minutes," she snapped after climbing off the boat in the most klutzy way and slowly lifting herself to a standing position. She squared up to me with a challenge in her glare. The blob of black and white bird poo was only inches from my face.

"I was going to tell you that... Well! A bird pooped on your head. It's... a big one." Instinctively she lifted her right hand to touch her hair. I grabbed her arm in mid air to prevent her from reaching the blob with her fingers.

"Aubrey, it's there. Do you have any tissues in your backpack?"

"Bird poo in my hair?" Her eyes darted upwards, though she obviously wouldn't be able to see the mess.

"Can't you feel it? It's... sitting there like a fried egg sunny-side up." I looked at my feet to stifle an oncoming outburst of laughter. Then, right there, out of the blue, Aubrey started howling with anger, threatening me with bulging eyes. I took a step back and stood petrified. Her fury had intensified from before. She ripped the zipper of her backpack open. It broke. Frantically, she began to look for tissues and found none. She lifted her backpack over her head and threw it at my feet with full force. I took another step back.

"Aubrey, I'll be over there," I pointed at a nearby bench. "You can join me when you calm down. I'll be looking for tissues in my backpack." I walked away from the situation, backwards as if not to turn my back on a fire. Eventually, I turned on my heels and quickly approached the saving bench. I breathed a sigh of relief and sat down. By now, Aubrey was in a forward bend, shaking her head from left to right. Maybe she was hoping the mess would drop out of her hair this way. But bird poop doesn't do that. It's made of different material, stretchy, sticky material. Again, I stifled a smile. I had found two packs of tissues in my backpack that would both be sacrificed for Aubrey's soiled hair. I decided not to hurry and offer my help. I waited on the bench, patiently watching her from a slight distance. Would I have to clean it up? I didn't want to think about it. My stomach somersaulted. "No, we'll find a musical bathroom," I said to myself. *The ones you can use for five minutes for a franc. They play music. After five minutes, the door opens automatically.* I smiled at the idea of timed musical bathroom use. *I won't be touching the bird poo. Not a chance.*

Eventually, Aubrey gave up the swinging motion in her forward bend, lifted herself, and took a few steps towards her backpack, which was still sitting on the ground where she had tossed it at my feet. With obvious resignation, she picked it up and investigated the zipper, eventually giving up on it. Slowly, she came towards the bench, the bird poop in her hair an even bigger mess than before. The swinging motion had visibly spread the poop throughout her hair. She had made it worse with the wrong attempt to get rid of it.

"Here," I said cautiously, holding out my two packs of tissues for her to use. She took them with hesitation and held her distance.

"Sorry," she mumbled. "It wasn't fair of me to yell at you. This mess isn't your fault. I just don't like it when people make fun of me." Hearing that last sentence, I deemed it wise to stay silent. "Can you help me clean it up?" This question was about to be raised. I took a deep breath. I was well prepared to give her my answer.

"Let's find a musical bathroom, or a Free Time. This mess needs a good rinsing." I waited.

"A musical bathroom?" Aubrey looked at me with big brown eyes.

"Yes, they come with a sliding door. It opens when you put a franc in the slot, and locks for five minutes when you are inside."

"What? Never heard of them." She glanced at me with an obvious air of wariness. "How do you know about them?"

"Rudi told me." I barely dared mention his name.

"Oh, yes! The drifter! He's still on your mind, isn't he?" There was another challenge in her tone of voice.

"Aubrey, let's go find a bathroom and clean up your hair. I still want to see Notre Dame today. Or it would be a waste of an afternoon." We stared at each other until she budged, bent down, and shouldered her backpack. We left the shore of the river Seine. The boat ride on this seven hundred and seventy-seven-kilometre-long river would be an unforgettable experience.

C H A P T E R

FIVE

NOTRE DAME

Solemnly, we approached Notre Dame on the small island called *Île de la Cité* in the middle of the Seine river in the fourth *arrondissement*. We stopped in our tracks in awe of the window glass art, the gargoyles, and the flying buttresses on the exterior. Then we entered through the main entrance to the west. Instantly, the cool and refreshing air flow enveloped me and invited me to proceed to the interior. This most famous of the Gothic cathedrals of the Middle Ages struck me as a triumph of French Gothic architecture, with magnificence apparent in all the details that surrounded us within this stunning structure. Aubrey had at once decided to explore the Cathedral from a different angle, back to front, unlike me, front to back, and opposite sides. I wasn't entirely sure how confident I felt about a separate exploration of Notre Dame since it was hard to locate anyone in the crowds. If I lost

Aubrey, I wouldn't find my way back to the hotel. I had no sense of orientation. I had never had the slightest sense of orientation.

"Back here at 04:00 p.m., Aubrey?" I stopped her in her tracks before she was out of sight. She turned my way and studied my face. It took her a long minute to respond.

"We have a tour in the Bell Towers at 04:15 p.m. Meet me at the front entrance where the tours gather. I'll be there at 04:00 p.m. Have fun!" Aubrey's facial expression changed to a huge grin. From furious to scornful, I had seen it all in one day.

"Well, then, enjoy your visit as well!" I felt defeated but didn't want her to pick up on my mood. So I turned around and went the other way.

***

During my solo tour, I found out that construction of Notre Dame began in 1163 and that it was completed in 1345. Notre Dame turned out to be a masterpiece of a cathedral within an almost two-hundred-year work span. I let this fact sink in as I realized an hour was gone. All at once, I felt a strong urge to sit down, rest, and feel the Cathedral's energy wash over me. I took a seat in a middle pew and began to watch the tourists for a while, until my mind's images conveyed to me the last important school event, the one that I would never quite forget or be able to forgive entirely. It was graduation day, just two weeks before Paris.

***

Out of the blue, my parents refused to come to the graduation ceremony that was to take place in the morning. The details of our disagreement had escaped me. Maybe it was the wrong response I had given to an issue. Maybe it had to do with my aquamarine dress. My mother and father had decided not to make an appearance for my once-in-a-lifetime graduation ceremony even though they were in the middle of getting ready for it when the argument between us started. I wasn't going to waste my time on it. In fact, I was ready, in my aquamarine dress, hair and make-up done, and decided to leave right away since I wasn't expecting them to change their minds about their abrupt decision. That meant no ride to school. The school was within walking distance. I had travelled to class on foot on those same roads for seven years. I'd be able to do it in heels. At the same time pumped and annoyed, I was on my way. After a huffing and puffing fifteen minutes, I arrived just in time for the speeches to begin. Unable to locate my closer school buddies in the crowd, I realized most of my fellow graduates were already there and seated. A little desperate, I managed to find a chair halfway up the audience from the stage — students, teachers, parents, and relatives — and sat down beside a fellow graduate, who used to be in my class, but whom I had always kept my distance from. She, Paige, was sitting with her friends and ignored me. I kept turning around to find Aubrey. In vain...

"Graduates, Ladies, and Gentlemen, we are gathered here at this outstanding school...!" My former math teacher, whose lessons I had never understood, was also the vice principal, and he began a speech that I had no nerve to listen to. My mind was elsewhere. His voice trailed into silence after about twenty minutes. I was uncomfortable about my quickly-upcoming stage appearance to receive my graduation paper and then face the whole crowd, students I liked, students I disliked, their parents, known and unknown to me, boys who used to have a crush on me, and a gazillion others. I felt ungrounded without support, no parents by my side, no friends...

My name was called, "Carielle Sander!" Hesitant, I cast a quick glance at Paige, who had just returned from the stage, vital graduation paper in hand. Her last name also began with the letter S. She was ahead of me in the alphabet. Paige gave me an absent-minded smile before turning away. She said nothing to me. My name had been called. My legs were wobbly. Everyone's eyes were on me as I was making my way to the front along the audience to the right. *Slow down! Walk with grace!* I felt nauseous. I saw the crowd in a haze. An invisible veil separated us. I had never been much for groups and crowds. Never mind facing one! Thankfully I didn't have to talk. I wasn't the top student of the year.

"Congratulations, Carielle! We are here to commend you on your excellent achievement over the last seven years at our school. Champion in foreign languages including Latin..." I no longer followed my former math teacher, Mr. Roberts, although my eyes were still glued to his mouth, which expressed my talents in descriptive words. I felt the urge to take an all-around glance at the crowd and turned towards the audience. I disbelieved the mass of people focused on me. My hands began to feel clammy and started to tremble, and then I discovered them. I couldn't trust what I saw, squinted and looked again while Mr. Roberts handed me my paper. In the last third of the audience, at the back so to speak, I spotted them, my parents. My mother! My father beside her, clearly not paying attention to his daughter's essential moments of graduation. My mother gave me a disinterested look with a strong touch of antipathy, and when she realized that I had spotted them, she turned to the left and looked out the window towards the schoolyard. My heart skipped a beat. I was unable to determine if it was for joy or confusion.

I left the stage and sat down again. Proud of my achievements, I looked at my paper, read the writing, felt the texture, smelled it as if I wanted to make it part of my being. Absent-mindedly, I smiled. I wiped a running tear off my cheek. After a long list of graduates, they had finally reached students with the letter W.

"Benjamin Wagner!" He instantly stood up and flew towards the stage, where similar words of applause for his particular talents were addressed to him. I looked at my hands. They had written so many school papers, especially in English and French. Before I managed to look at the stage again, I heard the noise of chairs scraping along the floor. Everyone was getting up and beginning to look for and to mingle with family and kindred fellow students. Realizing I was the only one still sitting, I stood up and began to search the crowd. I took furtive glances in all directions. I didn't spot my parents. I didn't see Aubrey.

"Who are you looking for?" Mr. Roberts tried to get my attention. With two big strides, he had come awfully close.

"Oh, Mr. Roberts... I am looking for Aubrey," I lied. "Have you seen her?"

"I am afraid I haven't. Will you be at the graduation party tonight?" His intense look caught me off-guard. Of course I would be.

"Yes... I will be at the graduation party tonight." I sounded too quiet.

"Looking forward to seeing you this evening." Mr. Roberts turned on his heels and disappeared in the crowd before I had another chance to say a word of appreciation for commending me on my foreign language skills in front of everyone. There I was, still standing beside my chair, unable to figure out the direction for my next step. No one was paying attention to me. *Well, then, why don't I... Where would I find Aubrey? No, no, where would I find my parents? Yes, my parents... Are they not looking for me? If the three of us were looking for each other, we would've already...*

***

"Carielle!" Someone was shouting. "Carielle! Carielle! Hey! Wake up! The Bell Towers! Our tour starts in five minutes." Aubrey's face appeared an inch away from mine when I opened my eyes and realized I was still sitting in the same pew at the Cathedral of Notre Dame. "I can't believe you are asleep with your head hanging off to the side. Isn't this a bit uncomfortable? Let's go!" In silence, and somewhat in a trance, I got off the pew and followed Aubrey to the main entrance where the tour was about to begin. She turned around often to make sure I was following her. I eventually held on to Aubrey's shouldered backpack as hundreds of tourists appeared to be passing by me as indistinct clusters of bobbing heads. If I had been one step behind, Aubrey would've been out of sight.

THE BELL TOWERS

"As you can see, *Mesdames et Messieurs*, Notre Dame de Paris has two Bell Towers, the North Tower and the South Tower. The North Tower holds eight bells. The South Tower is the one we find ourselves in right now. It is slightly smaller than the North Tower and holds the two largest bells." The tour guide, dressed like the Hunchback of Notre Dame without the hump, boomed with a roaring tone of voice inside the Towers. He led the tour in English with a strong French accent. Aubrey, myself, and the other visitors were standing with shoulders touching bare shoulders in the afternoon heat. Even in the dim Bell Towers the summer temperatures could be felt. No one bothered with light jackets, and no one was able to move an inch unless the whole group moved in unison. Sweaty skin was sticking to sweaty skin, and there was no way of getting away from it during the tour.

The South Tower was dark and oppressing, and at the sight of the largest bell, I couldn't help but wonder how a bell of that size and weight wouldn't just crash down to the ground. I couldn't imagine myself lingering underneath it. The *'Bourdon'* was quite important, as we learned.

"Notre Dame has ten bells all together. The *'Bourdon'* is the heaviest bell that produces the lowest tone. It dates back to the fifteenth century. King Louis XIV named it Emmanuel." The tour guide paused importantly.

"Carielle, what does *'Bourdon'* mean?" Aubrey whispered.

"It means… Let me find it in my dictionary." I quickly flipped through the pages in my travel dictionary, which I carried in the back pocket of my jeans every day during our stay in Paris. "It means something like a drone in Old French. It appears to be a musical term, of which I understand nothing," I concluded and admitted. Tour guide Hunchback continued…

"Emmanuel is indeed the largest, oldest, and most well-known bell here at Notre Dame's Cathedral."

"When was it cast?" Someone wanted to know. I perked up.

"Emmanuel was cast some time around 1680. He is considered one of Europe's finest bells. In 1944, he was designated a national historic landmark when he rang during the liberation of Paris from German occupation." Silence followed the mention of the end of World War II.

"Can you ring Emmanuel?" Another, younger tourist asked. The Hunchback started to laugh. With a bemused smile, he answered the teenager.

"Emmanuel would be ringing many times every day. It is not possible — sadly. Emmanuel only rings on special occasions. I can ring one of the smaller bells in the North Tower. Come with me!" The group began to move, whispering excitement and holding their breath in anticipation.

The Hunchback paced ahead with a quick step and stopped abruptly in front of the eight bells of the North Tower with the group of tourists right on his heels.

"Here they are," he thundered, "the smallest on one end, the biggest on the other." He turned away from the mumbling group to approach the smallest bell. With one quick strike of the drumstick in his right hand he made the smallest bell sing. The sound was deafeningly shrill and loud and definitely impressive enough for everyone to watch with their mouths wide open. The Hunchback smirked. "This is the highest-pitched voice of our Lady of Paris, as Parisians call 'Notre Dame' in English." His smirk broadened. "Feel free to look around this marvelous North Tower. Please don't touch the bells. We have a few minutes to spare here."

I followed Aubrey to the largest bell of the small ones, and we both stared at it. I took a closer look at its material and texture.

"*Quelle merveille, n'est-ce pas?*" I was caught off-guard by the deep — by now familiar — voice that had addressed me from the left. The Hunchback was standing right beside me with a grin. "*Vous êtes de France, vous et votre amie?*" He waited politely for me to respond without taking his eyes off my surprised glare. Aubrey looked at him as if he was none of her concern, then turned to the second biggest bell for inspection.

"No, I mean, yes, it's wonderful, and no, we're not from France. Germany!" I sounded like I wasn't at all prepared to have a conversation with the Hunchback.

"*L'Allemagne! Vous parlez français?*"

"*Oui!*" I wasn't sure what else to say.

"Are you aware of the historical facts of Notre Dame?" He switched to English.

"Some." I kept going with my one-word responses.

"Let me tell you..."

"I am all ears to learn about this *monument merveilleux*. Please go ahead, and maybe Aubrey would appreciate some more information, too." I raised my voice towards Aubrey and poked her right arm with my index finger to get her attention. Looking annoyed, she turned around and directed her focus to the Hunchback.

"I have a question," she said. "What exactly is Gothic? Like a cathedral built in a Gothic style." She studied him, with eyes darting back and forth between his face and his outfit *à la* Hunchback.

"Gothic, yes! One sure sign of a Gothic cathedral is the large stained-glass windows. More often than not they are rose windows. Of course, window art is not the only symbol of a Gothic church. There's the pointed arches that you have seen on the inside and outside, the rib vaults, the flying buttresses and — all around — the ornate decoration." He was on a roll. "You see Notre Dame was the seat of the bishop, and, therefore, it was the most significant religious building in Paris."

"Interesting," Aubrey mumbled while taking another glance around the Tower we were in.

"What are other historical facts about Notre Dame, facts that date back longer than the recent past?" His knowledge had spiked my interest for more details.

"Well, do you know who founded Notre Dame?" He looked from one to the other and waited.

"No!" Aubrey and I said in unison. He smiled.

"It was Louis VII who founded it. He wanted Notre Dame to be a symbol of political and economic power. But not just that! Louis VII wanted it to be a symbol also of intellectual and cultural power in France and abroad."

"Abroad? Does that mean the rest of Europe?" I wanted him to clarify.

"Yes, for the most part." The Hunchback fell silent.

"Anything else we might be interested in finding out?" Aubrey asked him with a slight challenge in her voice, as if she questioned his knowledge. I took a quick glance at her hair, scanning the spot that had earlier been soiled by bird feces. It looked alright in the dimness of the Tower. As they say, appearances are deceiving, and I wouldn't spend a minute of my day with a bird dropping in my hair, rinsed or not.

"How does Napoléon tie into the existence of this Cathedral?" I heard myself say absentmindedly, with my eyes still on Aubrey's head.

"Napoléon, while you're bringing it up," the Hunchback responded, reflecting for a moment. "Yes, in 1804, Napoléon crowned himself emperor at Notre Dame. Also, an English king was crowned at Notre Dame, and I beg your pardon, I cannot remember his name or the exact date."

"I have never been able to remember historical dates except when I needed to for an exam," I revealed. "History wasn't one of my strong subjects. But I do see the value of it, and how it would be important for us, for society as a whole, to learn from historical events, and use the lessons to improve our future actions in order to make the world a better place."

"Quite so," the Hunchback concluded. "Last but not least, I appear as a historical figure, too, a fictional one. The author of *The Hunchback of Notre Dame* felt compelled to write his novel. So he created it with that specific title in 1831 to save Notre Dame from demolition. Do you know who he was?" He looked at us with big eyes. He waited.

"Victor Hugo!" Aubrey blurted out.

"You got it! Victor Hugo! The novel was a huge success, or I wouldn't have appeared as a representation of the Hunchback in our tour today. Anyhow, the novel resulted in a major restoration of this Cathedral. So thank you to Victor Hugo." The Hunchback remained silent for a few seconds. "I see that most of the tourists have left the Tower. I have another tour in twenty minutes. You girls enjoy your stay in this most beautiful city of France. Have a pleasant afternoon!" Aubrey and I nodded in unison.

"You as well," I called to him as he turned to leave. "Thank you for sharing your historical knowledge with us."

"*De rien!* Very welcome!" In a flash, the Hunchback was out of the North Tower and out of sight. One more glance at the eight bells, and it was our turn to leave, too. Free Time was on the list for another greasy dinner. Or maybe Aubrey wanted to go 'home' to the hotel and wash her hair. As it turned out, she was not in a rush...

SEVEN

A SURPRISE VISIT

When we got off the Métro after Notre Dame that evening and made our way through the Parisian jam at the Métro station, I spotted a young man behind a small, rectangular table. It had a glass jar for coins on it. A guitar was leaning against the one end of the table right by his side. A big bucket with a single bunch of tulips in it was sitting at the other end of the table. Was he selling bouquets? The guy was standing, thanking a man for dropping a bank note or two into his jar. I stopped and looked at him, trying to pinpoint his nationality. My closest guess was the Far East, but definitely not Africa.

"What's up?" Aubrey challenged me. I ignored her and approached him. She trailed behind me with a loud sigh.

"*Excusez-moi, vous connaissez Rudi?*" I sounded too quiet.

"Sorry," he said. "*Vous pouvez répéter?* Repeat, please!"

"Rudi, would you know him?" I studied his face. His big smile narrowed to a grin of surprise. My guess was he would realize I was determined to wait for an answer. I had all the time and patience in the world to wait during this odd trip to Paris. Reluctantly, he spat it out.

"Yes, I know Rudi!" He paused. "Can I pass on a message from you?"

"Oh, of course. Yes! Please tell him that Carielle says hi." I turned to Aubrey. She stood petrified. Her stare revealed nothing other than she wasn't with it. "So, yes," I directed my attention back to the guy after making sure Aubrey didn't care to say hi, "just hi from Carielle." He had spiked my curiosity. "Where are you from?"

"Bangladesh," he smiled. He quickly regained the position of asking the questions. "How would you know Rudi?"

"He helped us find a hotel accommodation. Our youth hostel was booked. So, yes, we needed a place to stay, needless to say, reasonably priced." I grinned at him. "Was nice meeting you. Take care!"

"You, too. I will contact Rudi."

"No need to contact him. Just say hi when you see him." He nodded, and I turned to join Aubrey for our short walk to the hotel. I had resolved I wouldn't be taking any gloom-ridden comments from her regarding this incident. She must've felt it. She said nothing until we reached our hotel room.

"Who's first at the sink? I need to wash my hair, too," I asked Aubrey after slipping into my comfortable, silky-feeling tracksuit.

"Go ahead!" Aubrey sat down on her bed holding the map of Paris. "What do you want to see tomorrow? Le Sacré Cœur? Or L'Arc de Triomphe? Or…"

"Le Sacré Cœur sounds good," I said, head down in the sink to run water over my hair. It was no piece of cake to wash my mane in a sink of a small size such as this one. Thankfully my strands were only shoulder-length for the summer.

"Le Sacré Cœur it is. I'll figure out right now how to get there." Aubrey was beginning to sound like a mathematician with me, right down to facts and basics. She murmured something about best Métro connections, and walking distances, and points of interest. I drowned out her mumbling by rinsing my hair. I barely had a towel thrown around my wet strands when — out of the blue — the hotel phone rang in our room. As if a shotgun had gone off, Aubrey dropped the map. It fell to the floor. I stared at her, wide-eyed, and didn't move. The phone rang again.

"Pick it up," Aubrey commanded me. "You're the one who speaks French." I hesitated. Aubrey, not usually the one to be quick on her feet, jumped off the bed, lifted the receiver, and dragged it all the way over to where I was standing glued to the floor. She put the receiver in my hand.

"*Allô, allô,*" the voice paused. "*Allô?*" I finally lifted the receiver and held it against my right ear. I decided to respond, feeling apprehensive.

"*Bonsoir! Comment puis-je vous aider?* How can I help you? This is Carielle Sander." I turned towards Aubrey. "Hey, Aubrey, what's our room number?" I was still speaking into the mouthpiece.

"*Oui, Carielle, il y a un monsieur à la réception qui voudrait vous parler.*"

"Someone is… at the reception… for me?" I knew it was not Alexandre on the other end of the line. The voice was too deep to be Alexandre's. "Well, it's ten-thirty at night. Who is it? Can you send him up?" Aubrey shot me a furious look that struck me like a flash of lightning. "I would prefer staying in my room at this hour," I said.

"*Non, non, non, il ne peut pas monter à votre chambre. C'est interdit.*"

"Oh, he can't come up. Why not?" I wanted to know.

"Get down there and talk to him." Aubrey commanded me again. "Not a single guy will come up to our hotel room. I can tell you that."

"Hey, *Monsieur,* I'll be right down." I hung up the phone.

"Who is it?" Aubrey wanted to know. "The guy from Bangladesh?"

"How could it be him? I didn't give him my full name. I didn't give him the name of the hotel."

"How should I know what you guys talked about at the Métro station?"

"You and I, we both know who it is." I said, wrapping the towel around my hair a little tighter.

"Are you serious?" Aubrey challenged me. "You're going to the reception with a towel on your head and in your tracksuit?"

"I sure am dead serious!" I took two big strides to the door, opened it, slammed it shut behind me, and took the stairs down to the main level.

***

My step slowed as I reached the bottom of the stairs. I adjusted the towel that was draped over my hair. I took a furtive glance towards the reception area. There he was, Rudi. He was standing in front of the reception counter with what appeared to be an expectant look towards the staircase. His glare revealed nothing, not even in regards to my appearance. He smiled. Then he grinned.

"Rudi! Hi! Nice to see you! What has brought you here at this advanced hour?" I waited, scanning his face. He brushed his facial stubbles with the back of his right hand and appeared reflective. Then he stifled a laugh.

"Are you alright?" Out of the blue his gaze became intense and serious. He waited, refraining from rephrasing the question or repeating it. I was bewildered.

"Alright? Why would I not be? I just washed my hair, as you may guess. We visited the Eiffel Tower yesterday and Notre Dame today. We're planning...!" Rudi interrupted me.

"I am not asking about your sightseeing adventures."

"Oh, well... Yes, we are... quite alright. How are you doing? Why don't we talk upstairs?"

"Carielle, I cannot go up to your hotel room in this accommodation. It is run by Moroccans, and they won't have it — needless to say."

"Understood! Well, what shall we do? It's too late to go out or hang out. But you've come all the way, just like that." I felt bad for his efforts.

"Not just like that," Rudi responded drily with a sad expression on his face. "Kamal contacted me and suggested I'd check up on you."

"Kamal?" I briefly did some brainstorming and came up with absolutely no one. "Who is Kamal?"

"You met Kamal today at the Métro station. You were the one approaching him with the question if he knows me..."

"Oh, yes, well, he didn't tell me his name. He said he is from Bangladesh. How did he manage to get in touch with you so quickly?" Rudi just nodded slightly and looked reflective again but didn't answer my question.

"Listen, have you been raped?" With that question... hanging in the air, there was an uncomfortable pause between us. My eyes fell on the receptionist behind the small counter who had phoned us upstairs. He appeared to be busy organizing and stacking paperwork. Rudi had stressed every word in this last disconnected question, not the least bit concerned about his surroundings, nor taking his eyes off me. Neither had he bothered lowering his voice. The towel that was loosely wrapped around my hair fell to the carpeted floor. I stood there with my unkempt lion's mane feeling embarrassed. I felt my cheeks blushing, and took a quick look around, forgetting for a moment that we were speaking German. None of the Moroccans still in the TV room would know German, I assumed. With that in mind I regained my composure.

"No, of course not!" I replied under my breath, then smiled uneasily. "What would make you assume such a thing?"

"It's not uncommon for beautiful young ladies to get raped in the metropolitan of Paris. I just wanted to make sure. Believe it or not, I came all the way from Versailles to see... you for... that... worry. It was a hell of a trip."

"Versailles?" I couldn't believe my ears.

"Versailles! I had a super lucky streak today. Tourists from all over were handing me generous banknotes. It was an incredible day. But I left early to make sure you're not..." He turned his gaze towards the floor, bent down, and picked up my towel. "Here," he said, handing it to me. In slow motion, I took it. "Would you be alright stepping outside with me for a moment?"

"I think so," I replied a little too fast to a guy I had just met a few days ago, on top of it, under bizarre circumstances. I didn't have the slightest idea about him and his life, but for some reason I trusted him blindly. I turned around to take a look at the staircase.

"Don't worry about your friend. She's too scruffy to be in danger. Let's step out." He turned towards the front door without another word. I took one more glance back at the staircase and deliberately ignored the receptionist. I followed Rudi out the door.

***

As soon as we were out on the sidewalk in close proximity to the hotel entrance, Rudi used both his hands to begin searching his shirt pockets and then his jeans pockets.

"What are you looking for?" I asked curiously. I had missed a split second of it. An unlit cigarette was already hanging out of his mouth.

"Can't find my lighter. But it's somewhere. I know I have it." Rudi finally pulled his lighter out of a jeans pocket near his left knee. He lit up with visible craving for a smoke long overdue.

"Gauloises," he pointed out with importance. He took a long drag and blew the grey smoke past my face. "Here, try it!" He handed me the cigarette. I took it without hesitation for a taste of a strong Gauloise and started coughing right after my first and only drag. To my big surprise, Rudi began to howl with laughter. He didn't care to keep it down.

"My oh my, Rudi, I bet you Aubrey can hear you, to say nothing of the rest of the sleeping street." I coughed the words out more than I formed them. Rudi laughed even louder than before. I had tears in my eyes from the thick smoke when I handed him his cigarette back. "No, thanks, Rudi. I have my own, upstairs."

"Which brand?" He was teasing me by blowing more thick grey smoke past my face. Again, he grinned for a second and then howled with laughter. I was beginning to feel uncomfortable.

"Tone it down, or the receptionist may just kick me out of the hotel tonight. I'll have nowhere to go." I cautioned him.

"Then you'd come with me." Rudi turned serious as quickly as he had turned comical. I scanned his facial expression a little too long. All of a sudden, I had this strong urge to ask him where he lived, but I bit my tongue and remained silent. Maybe I didn't want to know. Maybe I was afraid of being lied to. Maybe I wouldn't know what to say if he told me he lived in a tent at the edge of the forest like an outlaw.

"Lord!" I answered looking at his feet.

"Lord what?" He appeared puzzled.

"You asked me what brand I smoke. I smoke Lord Extra."

"I have never seen you smoke."

"You have only known me for a day and a night, I mean, a few hours tonight, Rudi." I stumbled over my own words and felt embarrassed about the implication. "I smoke very little, a cigarette or two a day. Aubrey doesn't like it when I light up in her presence."

"Who cares about Aubrey!" Rudi said carelessly. I checked my watch. It was twenty minutes to midnight. The sky was a starry deep dark blue.

"What a mild summer night! The temperate air is what I miss during our sizzling hot days in Paris." I turned reflective. "Rudi, what exactly did you want me to come out here with you for?"

"First of all, I don't like hanging out around hotel receptions. Secondly, I needed a Gauloise. Last but not least..." Rudi didn't finish his third reason and stared down the street. His mind appeared to be in faraway places. "Okay, so..." He began solemnly only to eventually make a statement with emphasis. "As I said earlier on, I've had a hell of a good day in Versailles. I am planning to keep some of the dough for your and Aubrey's last vacation day in Paris. I would like to take you and her, for that matter, to a nice Parisian restaurant for dinner." He paused and then continued, "it's an invitation. You won't have to pay a cent."

"Our train leaves at night," I finally responded, deep in thought. My mind wandered off to a potential plan for the last day in Paris. The last day was still open. In the blink of an eye, I decided time needed to slow down.

"We can go for dinner before your departure," Rudi interrupted my contemplation. "Better yet, we can spend the whole day together. I'll pick you up here, at the hotel." His idea floated around the air above us.

"How would I let you know? I'll need to talk to Aubrey." I looked at him trying to figure out what the best course of action would be.

"Just say yes, and she'll tag along." Rudi howled with laughter at his suggestion, and I started laughing, too. Then we heard a noise, and I jumped at the squeaking sound of the front door opening. Rudi looked startled and stood frozen.

"There she is. We can ask her right now." A frightened Aubrey stood in the door frame.

"Come here," Rudi commanded. Aubrey stepped closer. "No need to be shy. We have a question for you."

"I just came to check up on Carielle," Aubrey sounded small. She pulled her pyjama shirt up to her nose and covered it just as Rudi puffed out some more smoke past my face. Aubrey started coughing. I looked at Rudi. I had expected another outburst of loud laughter, but Rudi stifled it at Aubrey's discomfort and awkwardness.

"Can we spend our last vacation day in Paris with Rudi?" Without beating around the bush, I blurted it out. Aubrey's face went milky white. She turned on her heels and ran to the hotel entrance, yanked the door open and — unmistakably — slammed it shut with full force.

"There, Rudi, you've got your answer." I whispered into the night.

***

"So, yeah," I said awkwardly. Rudi wore his most serious face imaginable.

"When is your last day?"

"July nineteenth, Thursday!" His right hand fell lightly on my left shoulder.

"I'll be here to pick you up, including your abominable friend Aubreyeyeyey." Rudi butchered the outgoing vowel sound of Aubrey's name in all seriousness. It made me smile and shake my head at the same time. I was very conscious of Rudi's hand still resting on my shoulder.

"What time?" I obviously needed to know that.

"In the morning." Rudi removed his hand.

"In the morning? Give me a time between eight and noon, or seven and eleven!" I waited. He shook his head. "What if you can't make it?" All those questions piled up in my mind waiting to be asked and answered... His body language wasn't the least bit revealing.

"I can make it. Trust me."

"How will you get home from here?" This question undoubtedly interested me the most. Would he maybe finally tell me where and what home was to him?

"I am taking the last Métro... In exactly thirty-five minutes."

"You must know the Métro system well." This was another implication on my end. "Tell me more."

"On the nineteenth!"

"What if you can't... come?"

"I'll call." Rudi had already stepped away by then and stopped on the corner about to disappear from view, when his words echoed down the cobblestoned street to me, me with my hands on the door handle to the hotel entrance. His last and loudest howl of laughter eerily sounded through the night. "Don't forget to brush your hair!"

"Thanks for reminding me," I whispered into the darkness with a grin on my face. I went inside with the towel loosely hanging around my shoulders.

EIGHT

LE SACRÉ CŒUR

When I entered the hotel room, all was dark. Aubrey had gone to sleep. I felt bad for having to turn the light on above the sink. My hair was a hopeless mess of dry tangles. I tossed the towel on the rack and began the tedious, long job of brushing my strands. I realized the sink hadn't been used. Everything sat there the way I had left it. *She didn't wash her hair?* I checked again. My shampoo, my hairbrush, my conditioner. *How does a girl go to sleep with traces of bird waste in her hair for days on end?*

"Will you be long?" Aubrey's coarse whisper floated over to me in the dimness. "I need to sleep… with the lights off!"

"I'm sorry. I'll quickly brush my hair and my teeth."

"You could've done that hours ago." She sounded reproachful.

"I know. But I wasn't here. Sorry again."

"I did all the research for tomorrow's day trip to Le Sacré Cœur while you…" Her voice trailed off into silence. Was she falling asleep? *I know what you wanted to say…. While I was hanging out with the drifter.*

***

We were getting used to the daily rides on the Parisian Métro. The rumbling put me into a state of dozing. I hadn't slept enough. My mind kept going back to my brief interaction with Rudi. My thoughts were going in circles around my conversation with him. Still, I knew nothing about him. Would he be joining us on the last day of our stay in Paris? Would he be taking us out for dinner? How would I get it across to Aubrey that we'd be spending the last day with him? Why did I decide on this course of action disregarding Aubrey's apprehension around Rudi? Why did it matter to me? Would he be able to help us, or get us into trouble?

"Le Sacré Cœur is sitting on the hill of Montmartre in the eighteenth *arrondissement* of Paris," she shared after an eternity of silence between us, while yanking me out of my circle of thoughts about Rudi. I wanted to say 'tell me more' but instead I said nothing, slightly nodded, and stared out the Métro window at the pitchblack tunnel walls that seemed to zoom by at light speed. At our destination station, I stumbled out of the Métro. Aubrey grabbed my arm.

"Are you alright? You look hungover. If I didn't know for sure you don't drink, I'd be wondering." Aubrey was blunt. I had no energy to respond with a reason that didn't exist.

"Thanks, anyway," I mumbled, not looking her way.

As we approached Le Sacré Cœur from a distance, I stopped and marvelled at its white exterior. "Shimmering white," I exclaimed, and my mood was on the rise.

"There's an explanation for it," Aubrey volunteered cautiously. "The exterior is built with a specific white stone that doesn't get infiltrated by water. So when it rains, the white stone releases calcite. Calcite cleans the stone and keeps it white." End of the chemistry lesson, I thought, but didn't say it. We climbed the hill of Montmartre. With each step upwards, I felt more light-hearted, peaceful, and free. I spread my arms as if they were wings and turned myself around in circles. When I stopped twirling, I found myself standing next to... someone — an intriguing woman! Her colourful blanket was neatly spread out on the grassy hill. She sat with her legs crossed. Her many bracelets on both arms and hoop earrings jingled in the breeze. Her garments and accessories were bulky around her slim figure and just as colourful as her blanket. She looked up at me with a glare of expectation. Her skin was dark, her eyes almost black with blue eyeshadow powdered on her eyelids. Her sensual, cherry red lips, I was sure, had many stories to tell. Our eyes met.

"*Quoi?* What?" She sounded surprised and somewhat unnerved, maybe because I had almost twirled into her.

"I am sorry to invade your space. I didn't mean to. I was lost in the moment of dancing." I apologized. "We've come to visit Le Sacré Cœur, my friend Aubrey and I." I pointed out Aubrey who had moved on to the entrance of the Basilica without further adieu.

"Tourists come for Le Sacré Cœur in the first place, while they should be lingering around this hill, inhaling and absorbing the energy of Montmartre. It has much historical value. It used to be a place of worship in ancient times. I basically live here in the daytime." She lifted her face towards the cloudy sky and took a deep breath.

"Yes, I can feel a change of the energetic vibration right here. I feel light like a feather, carefree, and at peace." I closed my eyes for a moment. "Would you share some of Montmartre's past?" I opened my eyes and took a quick glance at the entrance to Le Sacré Cœur. Aubrey was gone.

"Your friend went inside. It's very dark on the inside; something you wouldn't expect looking at the bright exterior. I prefer staying outside." I looked up and saw big dark grey clouds swiftly moving by Le Sacré Cœur.

"Ominous!" I directed my attention back to the gypsy. "*Je suis Carielle d'Allemagne.* I am Carielle from Germany. *Quel est votre nom?* What's your name?"

"*Je m'appelle Yelena. Enchantée de faire votre connaissance.* My pleasure!"

"Are you from Egypt?"

"My ancestors came from northern India. There is much history about us, but I know no details," she paused and took a panoramic glance at Montmartre. "This site was considered holy in ancient times. It was a place of worship for the pagans long before the erection of Le Sacré Cœur. Gallo-Roman temples had been built here. They were dedicated to the planets Mars and Mercury."

"Why Mars and Mercury, and not Venus and Jupiter?" I was curious.

"In Roman religion and mythology, Mars is the warrior and the agricultural guardian. Mercury presides over financial gain, commerce, travel, and communication. Those two were essential to Roman life and survival." She smiled and bowed to me in her cross-legged position. Gracefully she stood up and, after a moment of reflection, went on sharing her knowledge about Montmartre. "You see, Montmartre was the city's highest point. Parisian believers came here to worship. They felt closer to the sky, to God, and ultimately to Heaven on this hill, this highest point. Also, the views of Paris have been no more amazing anywhere else than from this hill. Montmartre is still the second-highest point in Paris after the Eiffel Tower, that is with Le Sacré Cœur on it. The third highest worth mentioning is Montparnasse. The Eiffel Tower is three hundred metres high; Le Sacré Cœur is two hundred and thirteen metres above sea level, followed by the Montparnasse Tower at two hundred and ten metres. It's all in pamphlets for tourists like you." Yelena looked towards the entrance, then to me, then back to the entrance.

"How do you know so much about it?" I had been listening closely, not wanting to miss a syllable.

"Montmartre has been my point of interest since I came to Paris. I read books about it, so many in fact that I remember the details."

"But why Montmartre?"

"Because it's a holy site." Yelena sounded all exclusive about something inaccessible and hidden from the general visitor.

"It is a holy site, regardless of the presence of Le Sacré Cœur, the Sacred Heart of Paris?" I wanted to make sure I had understood.

"That's correct," she whispered. "Once your eyes adjust to the dimness, look at the ceiling when you walk in. It's spectacular!" Again, I glanced at the entrance. It was time to explore the interior rather than spending the afternoon talking about Montmartre to Yelena. I also needed to find Aubrey, who didn't appear to miss me. A sudden thought stopped me from moving along.

"Would you be acquainted with... You wouldn't know a man, a young man, maybe not that young..." I broke off mid-question.

"Sorry?" She looked confused.

"Never mind!" In the blink of an eye, I had swallowed my question about Rudi. After all, what did it matter if Yelena knew him or not? She waved goodbye.

"Stop by here any time," she called. Once I had skipped over to the entrance to the Basilica, I turned around and waved to her on my part. Making every step towards the entrance count, I entered Le Sacré Cœur. The slightly damp dimness of the interior hit me like a cool compress. My eyes immediately searched the ceiling in the entrance hall, as I stood in awe squinting to make sense of what was presented to me. This would indeed be one of the biggest mosaics in the world. There he was in all his glory, Christ on the ceiling of the entrance hall to Le Sacré Cœur. Barely audible, I whistled and let the image sink in.

The Basilica was fairly empty that afternoon. Aubrey appeared beside me before I set eyes on her in the dimness.

"This mosaic is from 1923," she said and continued,"it is the size of four hundred and seventy-five square metres. Mind-boggling, isn't it?"

"Sure is impressive! It was completed two years before my grandmother was born."

"It took thirty-nine years to build Le Sacré Cœur. It was first shown to the public in 1914." Aubrey had done her homework or joined a tour. In general, I just realized she was getting so much more out of this trip to Paris than I was, at least from a historical point of view.

"This means the mosaic was added later on," I concluded.

"To judge by the year, I would assume so," Aubrey said with her nose held high and with the air of a history teacher. "Once you're done here, let's go up to the dome," she suggested. "It's free, and offers a breathtaking view over Paris."

"As may be expected, you've already been up there, haven't you?" I began to move towards the staircase.

"Just briefly. I decided to come look for you since you can't find your way back to the hotel at the end of the day." She grinned. I ignored her provocation and began my ascent to the dome. "Or maybe *la bohémienne* outside could've given you directions." I turned around on the staircase and shot Aubrey with a look of warning.

"What's wrong with making new friends? Apart from sightseeing, I have come to Paris to practice my French!" Having made a statement, I took two steps at a time to make it up to the dome, leaving Aubrey to trail behind.

"Yes, I know." Aubrey sounded defeated, puffing. She reached the dome after me, breathing hard. "Le Sacré Cœur has a story about a significant bell, too, like Notre Dame." Aubrey exhaled. "It is one of the biggest and heaviest bells in the world that is accommodated inside this Basilica. It was dedicated to the sacred heart of Jesus."

"*La Savoyarde?* I have heard about it." I responded absent-mindedly while looking at a photo of a French-looking gentleman in the pamphlet that I had picked up at the entrance.

"Yeah! *La Savoyarde* was brought to Le Sacré Cœur in 1895. It was pulled by twenty-one horses. The horses dragged the monstrous bell to the top of Montmartre."

Aubrey had discovered that information in her pamphlet and was reading it to me.

"That must've been a feat for the horses." I was looking at Montmartre from the top of the dome, imagining that particular scene with the enormous bell on a carriage pulled by twenty-one horses. Then I turned to Aubrey to show her the photo of the Frenchman. "This guy designed and built Le Sacré Cœur." I pointed at his black-and-white photo. "His name is Paul Abadie. He had a flair for the Romanesque style and designed the inside and outside of this Basilica accordingly."

"By the way, the bell weighs nineteen tons," was Aubrey's response.

"Still on the bell?" I rolled my eyes into the distance and, immediately startled, detected the most ominously appearing thunderstorm clouds racing towards Le Sacré Cœur from miles away. "We might be stuck here for a while," I casually said to Aubrey, not taking my eyes off the sky. A quick glance to the hill of Montmartre told me Yelena was gathering her belongings to call it a day and leave for an unknown destination. She, too, had begun to watch the sky for signs of a storm. "Mars and Mercury may just pay us a thunderous visit," I murmured. I turned around to find Aubrey looking for something in her backpack, a snack maybe. She hadn't heard me. Fascinated, I went back to observing the clouds that slowly but surely crept closer to Montmartre. I noticed Le Sacré Cœur was just about dark on the inside. "Are we the only ones left here?" I asked Aubrey who was still backpack diving. She scanned the dome.

"We might be," she answered. She pulled out a snack pack of crackers and cheese. "Want some?"

"Sure. Thanks." Then I heard a first loud thunderclap in the distance.

***

Aubrey and I had both gone to bed early after Le Sacré Cœur. By now, we were overloaded on Paris sightseeing and information since we were both interested in as much detail as possible. When was a basilica built? Who built it? How was it built? What material did they use to build it? The ginormous bells were a miraculous subject of their own. Our next tourist attraction, as we had decided, would be L'Arc de Triomphe, which included La Place de l'Étoile, which included Les Champs Élysées.

I couldn't sleep and stared at the ceiling. The hotel was quiet. I could've heard a pin drop. I hadn't seen the Moroccans for a while. Needless to say, all of them were men. It was a blessing no one at the hotel had tried to approach us after the incident two nights earlier. Two young Moroccans had knocked on our door in the evening. I was sitting on my bed nibbling on a cheese cracker when we heard them outside the door. Aubrey jumped up and grabbed her pocket knife, which made me grin into the palm of my hand. In fact, she had now developed the habit of not going anywhere without her pocket knife. It had to be on her person within easy reach. She unlocked the door, grabbed the door handle, and, with full force of her arm, yanked the door open. There they stood, two of them, looking young, friendly, and reluctant, and, as might be expected, on a mission. They didn't move. One of them asked us a question. I couldn't discern what he wanted. Chewing my cracker bits, I didn't bother finding out. The answer was already no. Aubrey turned around and gave me a mystified look. For once, there was some nonverbal understanding between us. Eventually we both shook our heads to their uncertain invitation. They stood there, appearing hesitant to leave. Aubrey slammed the door and locked up. Then she took three steps towards my bed and, trembling with fear like aspens, insisted I'd call the reception to report the incident. I didn't argue and lifted the receiver instantly. Alexandre answered. I made it sound benign and laughed it off somewhat. The conversation was brief. I was dead-beat and had no interest in going on and on about it. After calling the reception, the incident was history to me.

"Are you awake, Carielle?" I perked up. I didn't expect Aubrey not to be sleeping.

"I am. Was just thinking about those two guys at the door the other night. We didn't even bother finding out what exactly they wanted," I trailed off. She ignored my comment.

"What did you end up doing after the graduation ceremony? I was looking for you. Was going to show you the flowers your mom gave me for my graduation." I stopped breathing and narrowed my eyes at the ceiling in the dark but did not move an inch in my bed at her innocent-sounding question. Why did she bring it up again in the middle of the night?

My mind – of course – trailed off again to that morning of our graduation ceremony. It had already been haunting me on and off during my stay in Paris, and Aubrey had just given me a reason to travel back in time once more to the recent past of school's ending days.

I had informed Mr. Roberts, my math teacher, I was looking for Aubrey, while in fact I was looking for my parents. After scanning each and every direction and not knowing where to turn, I eventually walked up the three steps at the far end of the entrance hall that would lead to a hallway of classrooms and to a staircase to the right to more classrooms on the second floor. Students and parents were gathered there, some in the company of long-term teachers, speaking fondly of the day's happy event with visible traces of relief and contentment on their faces. I was trying to be inconspicuous. I turned around towards the information board and saw her... My mother! No trace of my father! She was standing a few metres away with her back to me. She was holding a bouquet of peach-colored daisies pressed to her chest, my all-time favourite flower. Aubrey was just coming up the steps towards my mother, intentionally or unintentionally. My mother stopped short in front of her and then stretched out her right hand towards Aubrey, which Aubrey responded to in a politely proper way. From what I could see, she then received my mother's heartfelt good wishes for a successful graduation. They exchanged a few words. Even though I was close by, I was not close enough to understand what was being said. Every student, parent, and teacher around me was engaged in vivid conversation, which made it doubly hard to overhear anything important to my ear. My mouth dropped open when my mother open-heartedly handed the peachy daisies to Aubrey. Aubrey took a quick glance at the beautiful bouquet. Somewhat shy in her moves, she lifted her gaze up to my mother's face. To judge by her body language, she was uttering words of thanks to my mother for a thoughtful gesture such as being offered the daisies that, I was sure, were originally meant for me.

I stood transfixed, my eyes glued to the duo of mother and friend. The surrounding flurry of activity passed me by in a haze. The setting I was part of became indifferent to me, while my awareness of wanting to remain low profile stayed intact. For that reason, I snapped out of my frozen state, turned on my heels towards the stairs to the second floor, but quickly decided to hang right for a dash off the premises. Without turning around to see whether my mother and Aubrey had left the scene, I made my way out the other entrance door, the door I hadn't used to enter the school building earlier. I walked on to the schoolyard in an unassuming way while mostly keeping my eyes on the sidewalk in front of me. Anger was building up inside of me and would soon be bubbling and boiling over the top. I felt tears burning in my eyes. I hadn't run into a single familiar face by the time I reached the street and unintentionally found myself right next to Wilfred's silver-grey Jetta. He had just pulled up and parked.

"Hey, Carielle, do you want a ride to Lenora's house? She's invited all of us over for a drink of champagne." Wilfred locked his car while looking my way over the rooftop. He dropped his car keys into the right pocket of his black dress pants. I swallowed, glaring at the Jetta in front of me, then all of a sudden straightened up like a soldier and met Wilfred's gaze.

"When? Now? I'd like to join you." I sounded determined, though I felt impartial about a get-together at my homeroom teacher's house.

"It's thoughtful of her to invite us, isn't it? It may be the last time for her class of 1984 to be together." Wilfred was right, of course.

"I guess!" My response was lacking enthusiasm.

"What's wrong?" Wilfred's question was a sign he was tuning into my current mood.

"Oh, nothing, Wilfred! It's just... It is such an emotional day. High school is done after years and years of learning, studying, writing exams. And this building... will be... history." Wilfred had come around his Jetta and stood right in front of me now. Concerned, he scanned my face after throwing a quick glance at the backside of our school building.

"That's it, emotional about today?" He sounded in doubt. There was a pause, a second too long.

"Yes, that's it!" I said in a tone of voice that wouldn't leave him questioning my emotional state. Truth to be told, Wilfred knew me rather well. He wasn't just another classmate. We had often spent time together outside of school going for walks around his secluded residential area while pondering life.

"Let's go. I'll give you a ride home after Lenora's." Out came the car keys again. He opened the passenger door for me and went around the Jetta to the driver's side. I got in and found myself sitting beside him. It dawned on me that we hadn't been on a car ride together for quite some time. It felt familiar and comforting.

I was insecure about home and going home. *Do I really want to go home today?* I had to snap out of it.

"Yeah, let's go to Lenora's for a drink of champagne. It'll be fun. Thanks for the lift, Wilfred."

***

"Carielle? Did you hear me? Are you awake?" I finally heard Aubrey's low voice, very quiet, and the only sound in this blackened room where the blinds let no streetlight in from outside. I was sad about the crippling memory that Aubrey was part of. However, it hadn't been her choice to receive a gift from my mother, especially the gift that was meant for me in the first place. That was my assumption, and I wasn't about to verify it. Just because of a childish argument I had lost my mother's respect for me on graduation day. I turned over onto my right side in my bed to face Aubrey in the dark.

"Yes, I am awake." Silence followed. Was Aubrey surprised that I finally responded?

"What did you end up doing after the graduation ceremony?" She repeated the nonsensical question.

"I went to Lenora's house for a drink of champagne. With Wilfred." I sounded bored.

"Ah, with Wilfred…" Another minute went by, and she pulled her duvet up to her chin and began to snore within seconds. She was instantly asleep, breathing rhythmically. I lay awake for another hour at least. *Is this all she was waiting for, an answer quite short and to the point. No further questions… Hers must be a scientist's mind indeed. Here's the basic answer to her question stripped of all the trimmings. If that was me asking, I'd want to know much more. Maybe her mathematical mind made her the boring friend who she had been. It left no room for imagination. It left no room for dreams. Romance had never been a topic at all.*

I was longing for the friend I had been able to talk to about anything, but she had left the city for another destination four years earlier.

NINE

L'ARC DE TRIOMPHE

It was already early afternoon when we were taking a stroll along Les Champs Élysées the next day. Our final destination was L'Arc de Triomphe. The mid-July sun was burning brightly with a scorching temperature from above. Aubrey was wearing her sunhat. I had been a sun cell all my life and didn't mind the heat. There was one coffee shop next to the other on this famous street in Paris. Tourists were lined up for tables wherever I turned. I didn't feel like taking a snack break at any of the coffee shops on Les Champs Élysées and hurried along with Aubrey in tow.

"Hey, Carielle, what's the rush? We have lots of time to get to L'Arc de Triomphe. Let's stop for lemonade. There is a McDonald's in this underground passage. It will be cooler down there." Aubrey wiped her forehead with the back of her right hand.

"Would you like a tissue?" I challenged her manners with a repelled tone of voice.

"No, I wouldn't. I need lemonade." Aubrey didn't get my allusion. On this trip, I had learned that proper manners could not be taken for granted in others, including Aubrey.

"Lemonade? If anything, I'd like a real American coffee." I led the way down the stairs into the passageway. Aubrey followed. I opened the heavy door to McDonald's and then stopped abruptly. Not unexpectedly, Aubrey bumped into my back.

"Sorry about that," she mumbled. When I turned around, I saw her holding her nose. "I bumped my nose when I ran into you." *As if I couldn't tell...* When she realized I wasn't going to comment either way about this little mishap, she assured me. "It'll be alright."

"Okay then," I said under my breath, not wanting to spend any more time on this incident. I had expected an empty McDonald's since every other tourist appeared to be crowding around on Les Champs Élysées. No such luck! With a little bit of searching I spotted a table for four occupied by one young gentleman of African descent. Aubrey followed my gaze.

"Will you ask him if he would share his table with us?" Aubrey had guessed my intentions.

"I might, or we'll have nowhere to sit." Mindfully I approached our chosen table. "*Excusez-moi, Monsieur, voudriez-vous partager votre table avec nous?*" I waited.

CHAPTER

"*Oui, bien sûr, Mademoiselle. Venez-y!*" I smiled at him, then I turned to Aubrey. She was still holding her nose.

"He said yes."

"I'll go order lemonade and coffee for you. Cream and sugar? Do you want anything else?" Hastily, she offered to place our order with an air of true happiness.

"Coffee with one cream would be excellent. Nothing else. Thanks. I'll stay here to safeguard our two chairs." The guy looked at me, baffled. He obviously did not understand German. I was hoping he would leave. Reluctantly I sat down.

"Done deal!" Aubrey shouted with a tone of importance. "I'll be back in a few minutes; sooner than that if they don't speak English." Aubrey hurried away. It was the guy's turn now to smile at me. He made no effort to pack up and leave.

"*Vous êtes d'où?* Where are you from?" I had expected that question.

"*D'Allemagne.* From Germany. Here on vacation for a few days." It felt like I had repeated myself on several occasions. Therefore I kept my answer short. Or perhaps I didn't want to reveal more than I needed to.

"*Ah, d'Allemagne. C'est un pays merveilleux.* Beautiful country. Do all girls in Germany have blond hair, fair skin and green eyes?" I realized I must've come across as an example of a typical German girl.

"*Monsieur,* some have blue eyes. Some have light brown hair, fair skin and brown eyes, like my travel companion

Aubrey. Some have black eyes, just like here in France, or in Denmark, or in Austria…" The last thing I wanted was to delve into the subject of eye colour with this young guy in the middle of McDonald's off Les Champs Élysées while waiting for Aubrey to bring me my coffee. I smiled in return. With my long answer I wanted to assure him that I took him seriously, including his obvious allusion to my outward appearance.

"*Vous êtes étudiant?* Are you a student, *Monsieur?*" Awkwardly searching for something to say, I was going to sidestep a potential conversation about me… What could I ask him without appearing too personal?

"*Oui.* I often study at Le Centre Pompidou where I can find the right reference material for my assignments. Have you been to Le Centre Pompidou?"

"Not yet. I doubt we'll have enough time left on this trip to visit the… What is it called again? Centre…?" If I had seen it written down, I would've remembered.

"Centre Pompidou!" He smiled an even broader smile showing me his snow white teeth. "It houses a big library, so to speak, a treasure chest for university students. Besides that, if you like modern art, Le Centre Pompidou accommodates the largest museum of modern art in Europe."

"Oh, well, I am not a big fan of modern art. But we may as well check it out while we're here, time permitting that is. Thank you for sharing, *Monsieur.*"

"The building itself is modern art." He laughed. "I don't fancy it."

"Would you have a photo of Le Centre Pompidou?" Needless to say, I was curious now.

"*Pardon, non, pas de photos!*" He shook his head. A minute of uncomfortable silence followed.

"Where is Le Centre Pompidou?" I was determined to keep a conversation going that was neutral in its subject. Right then and there, I suddenly felt grateful to whoever designed Le Centre Pompidou.

"It's located in Beaubourg, fourth *arrondissement*. It's easily accessible from anywhere in Paris. You can take the Métro. The Métro is..." I interrupted him.

"Oh, I know. Aubrey and I have been taking the Métro most days to various destinations." I paused, caught off-guard by my own impatience. "Sorry about interrupting you. I didn't mean... to be impolite." His and my verbal exchange had come to a halt again but thankfully Aubrey showed up with our order.

"Carielle, your coffee is still on the counter. I couldn't carry it besides my lemonade, and... Can you go get it so my food doesn't get cold?" My eyes bulged at Aubrey's big order. There was a large plate of French fries and two juicy cheeseburgers with huge amounts of ketchup.

"You could've taken a tray," is all that came out of my mouth. I was still staring at her enormous dish.

"Allow me to get your coffee, *Mademoiselle*." For an instant I had completely forgotten about the guy at the table. Even though he didn't understand German, he would've caught on by observing my interaction with Aubrey.

"Thank you for offering, *Monsieur*. I am already standing. I don't mind getting it." I wasn't going to leave my coffee to a stranger. Before he could say another word, I had turned my back on him to quickly head to the counter.

***

It was mid-afternoon by the time we reached L'Arc de Triomphe on La Place de l'Étoile. Aubrey's stomach appeared to be so full from her late McDonald's lunch that she had slowed down our walk and our arrival. She had been putting one heavy foot in front of the other accompanied by laboured breathing. Her sunhat now hung off to the side. If there had been a taxi waiting along Les Champs Élysées, she would've talked me into getting a ride for the last kilometre. Time and again we had to slow down or take a short break. Finally L'Arc de Triomphe had come into view.

"Almost there, Aubrey," I cheered her on. There was a smile playing around my lips. I didn't want to come across upset about the delay. Aubrey used her last short break — so I was hoping — to open the map that she had been carrying in her left hand. The paper had become damp from her sweaty palms.

"You know," she chimed, "that La Place de l'Étoile is no longer called La Place de l'Étoile. La Place de l'Étoile is an outdated term. That square is named after Charles de Gaulle. Pardon my bumpy pronunciation. They renamed it. It is now La Place Charles de Gaulle."

"Well, in our French learning books it was always La Place de l'Étoile. It sounds a lot better, too." I made a point of defending the historical name.

"Our French books were beyond outdated and so hard to study from. Every chapter was a different historical event like Joan of Arc or even the festivals in France. Vocabulary for everyday communication was missing. This is one reason why my limited language skills cannot get me around Paris. My historical knowledge about Voltaire doesn't buy me a baguette." Aubrey looked at me with an air of resentment. I chuckled.

"I suppose you've got a point. So, why did they change the name? The name of La Place de l'Étoile, I mean? Does it say?"

"They changed it after Président Charles de Gaulle's death in 1970." Aubrey's eyes flew over the corresponding paragraph on the map.

"Oh, that was already fourteen years ago. It's been quite some time. Place Charles de Gaulle!" By sounding it out, I wanted to become familiar with it. The name of the former Président in Place Charles de Gaulle, however, was lacking spice in its sound vibration. Place de l'Étoile sounded magical, Square of the Star. *Yes, it's a star with L'Arc de Triomphe in its centre.* "How many avenues meet at L'Arc de

Triomphe, or, better said, go off it?" I was ready to take the map from Aubrey whose eyes were scanning the section about L'Arc de Triomphe.

"Twelve straight avenues," she announced, "and that includes Les Champs Élysées. Here, see for yourself." She handed me the map, all rolled up for easy stowing in a backpack's side pocket. I took it but didn't unfold it.

"I believe you, Aubrey."

***

"L'Arc de Triomphe de l'Étoile, here we are," I said cheerfully and turned to face Aubrey, "this is one of the most famous monuments of this charming city. Let's go inside, Aubrey. I hope we'll be able to see the twelve radiating avenues from above. It will be quite a sight."

"I think it would be wise to take a moment of silence when we enter to honour the tomb of the Unknown Soldier from World War I," Aubrey suggested cautiously.

"Not just the Unknown Soldier," I added, "but all French warriors who died for France in revolutionary wars." We went inside L'Arc de Triomphe and found ourselves in complete silence. No one else was present. The atmosphere invited us to spend a solemn moment that lasted a few minutes.

"Look at all the inscriptions, Aubrey!"

"They are the names of French generals and French victories. I noticed them on the outside, too." Aubrey's voice was no louder than a whisper. I decided to prolong my silence while making my way to the top with light, soundless steps.

"Is the tomb of the Unknown Soldier beneath the vault?" I needed some clarification on its location for the purpose of respect.

"Yes, it's under the vault." Aubrey confirmed my assumption. With snail speed we reached the top of L'Arc de Triomphe. Both of us took a panoramic look in continued silence until we moved on to cast a glance at the twelve radiating avenues. We proceeded counterclockwise to cover all the directions.

"This is phenomenal!" I exclaimed. "Square of the Star indeed!" The traffic on the twelve radiating avenues was magnetic to watch. We couldn't get enough of following vehicles driving away from La Place de l'Étoile on as many as twelve avenues. We extended our stay, at the same time taking a huge break from walking. By the time we decided to leave, it was late afternoon.

"As you can see by the setting sun, we are at the west end of Les Champs Élysées." Aubrey pointed out the direction without consulting her map after looking towards the sky. She unfolded her map to be sure her observation was correct.

"What's the best way of getting back to the hotel from here?" Needless to say, I had no clue.

"There's a Métro station close by. We'll go there rather than walking all the way back to where we got off. I am actually done with walking today, or better yet, done with it for the entire trip. I have never travelled this much on foot in my life." It sounded final.

"Our last day is here, anyway." I said it with hesitation since there was something about the last day she was still in the dark about. How would I get it across to her?

"So what do you want to do tomorrow on our last day? Why haven't we made any plans yet? There's Montparnasse. There's L'Hôtel des Invalides..." Aubrey looked straight into my eyes; she was no more than two inches away from my face.

"There's Les Catacombes," my mind trailed off into an image of piled up skulls. "Six million people's bones have their final resting place in Les Catacombes, including Robespierre's. Remember him from history class with Mr. Schultz? Robespierre was the radical democrat in the French Revolution of 1789. I only remember the year because of seven-eight-nine." I smiled away at my insufficient history brain.

"Yes, he was the reason for the Reign of Terror. Eventually, though, he was overthrown and arrested by the National Convention. Under Robespierre more than seventeen thousand enemies of the Revolution were executed by guillotine."

"A wicked era it was, for sure, back then." Historical times of much execution were always a reason for a moment of silence and contemplation, also between us.

"So what about tomorrow?" Aubrey insisted. I felt it wasn't the right moment to be upfront with her about including Rudi into our planning for the last day. I needed to keep it secret a little while longer.

"Let's figure it out at the hotel where it is quiet enough for me to hear myself think. Shall we... ?" Aubrey nodded, and we left L'Arc de Triomphe behind us.

***

We crashed as soon as we were through our hotel room door. The tourists, the Parisian traffic, the Métro, and the walking had made me so tired that I didn't bother changing into a comfortable outfit, my aquamarine jogging suit. I sat down on my bed, then instantly fell into a horizontal position, and, as might be expected, drifted off to sleep in split seconds. When I stirred, it was pitch dark outside. Aubrey had not drawn the blinds. When I turned away from the window, I saw she was frantically packing her belongings in the dim light of her flashlight. Maybe she didn't want to wake me and had therefore decided to leave the ceiling lights off.

"Done snoozing?" It was more of a statement than a question. "When are you planning on packing your stuff? It's almost eleven."

"I don't have much to pack. I only took out of my suitcase what I needed on a daily basis. I can pack that in the morning. Speaking of which, when do we have to be out of here?" All of a sudden, I remembered Rudi wanting to stop by to pick us up. I was instantly awake. My brain started doing flips around the time he wanted to be at the hotel. *Did he say seven or eleven?* My internal question remained unanswered. I just couldn't remember, and Aubrey interrupted me.

"Can you call the reception to find out when we have to check out? Maybe they don't have a check-out time because no one in their right mind usually stays in this dump, which means we might be able to leave our bags here until it's time to take the Métro to the train station. Maybe we can come back in the late afternoon to get our stuff. So can you call Alexandre? Carielle?" Aubrey stopped packing, stood there, and stared at me, obviously waiting for me to answer her. In slow motion, I got off the bed. Without looking at her, I walked over to the phone and grabbed the receiver. I dialled zero for reception.

"*Bonsoir, Alexandre! Quelle est l'heure de départ? Nous partirons demain matin.* We are leaving tomorrow." I listened with a sharpened sense of hearing. The line was staticky. Alexandre's voice was in and out. "*Répétez, s'il vous plaît.*" I waited. "Yes. Okay. That is very thoughtful of you. We appreciate it. Thank you." I hung up rubbing my eyes. I stared at the phone as if I had forgotten about something important.

"What did he say?" Aubrey stood right behind me. I turned to face her.

"He said we are welcome to leave our bags and suitcases in the hotel's baggage area for the day and pick them up before we go to the train station if it's not a detour." I yawned into her face to make her aware she was standing too close and occupying my personal space.

"I told you," Aubrey sounded smug, "that the hotel has no guests other than the Moroccans. It's empty. No one wants to board in this dumpster." She took a huge bite of her mini pepperoni stick and began to chew with her mouth wide open. I was repulsed watching the pepperoni go to bits and pieces between her teeth and her tongue.

"Will you excuse me, Aubrey? I... I... I will need to go down to the reception to... clarify something." I could've kicked myself for being so bumpy in my expression.

"Call back! The phone's right in front of you," she commanded.

"Actually, no. I won't be talking over the phone again. The phone line is very staticky. I could barely understand Alexandre. I will do this in person. Excuse me, will you?" Not about to wait for another comment from her, I managed to step between corpulent Aubrey and her messy bed that had a mountain of blankets and clothes piled up on it. There were hotel items mixed with her personal items on, around, and under the bed. I jumped over her runners by the door and switched on the ceiling lights. "I'll be back in five minutes." In the blink of an eye, I was through the door crack. From the hallway I closed the door. It clicked shut. Then I straightened myself up and stopped for a moment to check myself over. Luckily, I was still wearing my blue jeans and my black-and-white panda bear shirt from our earlier outing. I decided I looked dressed acceptably enough to run into other, most likely male, hotel guests.

"Alexandre, *bonsoir!*" I called from the bottom of the stairs as the reception came into view. I was out of breath by the time I reached the reception counter. There he was, Alexandre organizing piles of paper while on the phone, listening. He gave me a sign to wait a moment. I stood there, impatience slowly creeping up my spine. After endless minutes he finally hung up. I moved closer to the reception counter.

"What can I do for you?" His eyes looked heavy with fatigue. His voice sounded sluggish. He yawned into the palm of his right hand. "Sorry, it's been a long day."

"Will you be working all night?" I felt empathetic towards him and would have wanted him to get some rest.

"No, my dad will be taking over around midnight." Alexandre looked at the oversized brass clock on the wall behind him. He yawned again.

"I'll make it quick. Remember that guy... who came by here a couple of nights ago?" I held my breath with excitement to see his response and hear the answer. Alexandre frowned.

"Oh," he said, "yes, of course! Rudi! He used to be a regular here. I do not know him well, but some of our residents do." Alexandre paused as if it was my turn to speak.

"Residents?" Curiosity won over excitement. "What residents?"

"Some of the Moroccans you met in the TV room the other night live in this hotel. Some have been here long-term. In fact the majority of them live in our accommodation long-term." Alexandre looked at me with intense brown eyes. Maybe he was curious about my response to this statement. I took a step back. I tried again, sort of from scratch, not having expected the detour.

"So does Rudi visit them?" At this point my brain began to throw me into a loop of innumerable questions. They kept coming around in a circle one by one, urging me on to ask them. It was overwhelming. But I said nothing else at first. My mouth was incapable of forming the necessary words in the right order. I stammered, stressing every word. "Does he have... business dealings with them?" Alexandre opened the filing drawers under the reception counter to accommodate the piles of paper. He picked up the first pile.

"*Pardon?*" He was buying time. It was obvious. "Business dealings? Not that I know of. You would have to ask the Moroccans." Alexandre did not look at me. He was a little bit too focused on the piles of paper. He placed the first pile in the drawer to the left and closed it gently. Then he eventually looked up at me with the same intense brown eyes. "Are Rudi's activities the reason why you've come down? Are you hoping for information from me? I will not be able to assist you. Just because he is a regular at this hotel doesn't mean I know about his life. I don't. Sorry, Carielle." There was a moment of uncomfortable suspense.

"Well, no, I haven't come down to ask you about his life. I was going to ask you if he called... today?" Somewhat self-conscious about my question, I gazed at the brass clock as if the answer might appear on the face of the clock. Alexandre's smile was barely noticeable and was gone in the blink of an eye. He rested his forearms on the counter, his face moving a little bit closer to mine.

"No, he didn't call. Were you expecting him to call you?"

"Yes and no. It's just that..." Would Alexandre really need to know the details?

"Do yourself a favour, don't hang out with Rudi if you value your safety." Hearing Alexandre's good advice, it instantly struck me that he had revealed too much. With the speed of light he added, "Speaking of your departure, when would you like to pay for your stay?" I had to switch gears. The change of subject caught me off-guard.

"Tomorrow before we leave," I said apologetically, spotting a shadow behind the reception out of the corner of my eyes. Alexandre's dad's face partially came into view and vanished again from sight just as swiftly. Getting slightly uncomfortable around father and son, I decided it was time to go. I had my answer. Rudi had not called. What more could I ask? "*Bonne nuit, Alexandre. Merci!*" The words tumbled out of me before I could think of them. I turned towards the staircase and quickly made my way upstairs in the dim lighting of the hotel corridors. *I guess he will be here tomorrow morning. At some point... Now to Aubrey...*

***

"So? What's taken so long? Did you pay for our room?" I hadn't expected Aubrey to still be awake. It appeared she had been waiting for me to return so she could be on me like a hawk. I had hoped to be on my own with my thoughts and contemplations while getting ready for my last night in this hotel bed. Even though I was annoyed, I answered Aubrey calmly.

"I haven't paid for our stay yet. I told Alexandre the charges will be taken care of tomorrow before our departure." I had a faint hope Aubrey would be satisfied with my response.

"Then, if I may ask, what did you go down to the reception for?" She challenged me with a demanding tone of voice. Was she on an investigatory mission of some sort? Why did it matter? *You may not ask.* In no time at all did I need to come up with a plausible response that did not reveal the actual reason.

"I didn't spend much time at the reception," I said loud and with conviction. "I needed some fresh air. I... also needed a cigarette. You know that I smoke on occasion." I pretended to look for my pyjamas under the bed covers while coming up with this pretext, knowing fairly well that my pack of cigarettes had been left at the bottom of my backpack.

"You left the hotel by yourself? It was dark." I had guessed she wouldn't buy my ruse.

"Yes. I was right outside the entrance."

"And?" She sat down on her messy bed and waited.

"And... nothing! Let's get some sleep. It'll be a long day tomorrow and an even longer night on the train," I concluded. I jumped into my pyjamas and immediately marched over to the sink to wash my face and brush my teeth, so she would no longer be able to continue her interrogation. The thick air in our hotel room was the reason I voluntarily missed my chance to talk to Aubrey about spending our last day with Rudi. After all, he was the reason for the secrecy in the first place. *I'll mention it to her in the morning. Once Rudi is here, there won't be much she'll be able to do about it.*

"Les Invalides, Montparnasse, or Les Tuileries tomorrow... or Les Catacombes?" Aubrey obviously didn't respect my bedtime. I was about to drift off to sleep. I ignored her by pulling the bed covers up to my chin. "What time do you want to get out of this dump?" I barely heard 'get out' and 'dump', a word she had been using frequently to characterize this hotel.

"At eleven," I said and was gone.

LAST DAY
IN PARIS

The brightness of the room woke me around eight. I blinked and swallowed at the thought of spending a last morning in this hotel and a last afternoon in the capital of France, by far one of the most historically attractive cities in the western world. Needless to say, I would not be missing our hotel room much. However, it had made it possible for us to stay in Paris for a few days rather than taking the train back to Germany in the evening after our arrival. Thanks to Rudi, we had been able to live our planned vacation. The drifter had saved the day, which put a smile on my face. It occurred to me that I had not yet wondered about missing Aubrey's presence or missing spending entire days with her in a foreign country. Would I want to go on a holiday with her again? Right then and there I wasn't sure. I felt myself getting anxious about starting the last day and sat up in my uncomfortable hotel bed.

"Aubrey, are you awake?" I heard a very quiet snore from the bed next to mine. Since I had no clue about the time of Rudi's arrival, I needed to try my darndest to drag our departure out until eleven so we wouldn't miss one another, Rudi and us. Better said, Rudi and I. Aubrey, I was sure, could do without him. I stayed in bed, turned away from the sunlight, and — with a sense of desperation — tried to pinpoint my obsession with Rudi. At first, it failed. He was not my type. His outward appearance did not attract me. He was too short, though his curly light-brown hair was somewhat cute. I really didn't enjoy the way he conversed. He was somewhat loud. His laughter sounded obnoxious. Yet, he had some inexplicable power over me, one of magnetic attraction. The reason for it had to be the mystery of his personality. No matter what and how much he revealed — if anything — I ended up knowing him no better than before. There was more. I was drawn to his street smarts and the way he swiftly moved about, unnoticed. Paris appeared to be in his very being and had become part of his essence. What an unusual way of life he had chosen. Or maybe it had chosen him.

Staring at the ceiling, I became aware of my heavy eyes. I fell asleep for what seemed like seconds, only to be woken by Aubrey at a quarter after nine.

"Carielle, get up! I want to be out of here by ten. Let's make the most of our last day in Paris." In slow motion, I began rubbing my eyes and stretching in bed.

"Ten?" I mumbled. "What's the rush? The room is ours until eleven."

"Why would you want to spend more time than necessary in this run-down establishment?"

"I just wanted to sleep in," I lied. "I am anticipating a sleepless night on the train."

"Well, me, myself, and I want to leave." She sounded on the brink of a nervous breakdown. "I never had a chance to call my parents. They still don't know how I've been."

"You'll be home tomorrow morning, Aubrey." I jumped out of bed and started packing my few things in a specific order, which took up more time. As always, I applied a little make-up in a meticulous way. Aubrey was sitting on her bed breathing hard, staring down at her hands in her lap.

"Aubrey, why don't you go... Never mind!" It was ten-thirty. I was speeding up. At ten to eleven, the hotel room door clicked shut behind us. We went downstairs and paid for the room. At eleven, we found ourselves outside the front entrance. Alexandre had agreed to keeping our luggage for the day.

"What now?" Aubrey asked. I kept looking up and down the street in an inconspicuous way hoping to see Rudi coming towards us, so to speak, out of the backwoods. But he was nowhere to be seen. I scanned the corner down the street where he had disappeared from view a few nights ago when we last talked. *Just as well, I never told Aubrey we'd be spending the last day with Rudi. We obviously won't be.*

"Just a sec, Aubrey!" I ran back inside without waiting for Aubrey's reply. Alexandre was busy helping a new guest. I stood in line, anxious. I began to twirl my long strands of hair as a result of my sudden nervousness. I looked back towards the entrance expecting Aubrey to emerge at any moment. So far, she had not.

"*Une minute, s'il vous plaît, Alexandre!*" I called after him as he turned his back on me to leave the reception area. The new Moroccan guest had disappeared into the staircase. Alexandre was about to follow him. "Alexandre!" I had taken some steps towards the staircase but decided not to go up. Maybe he was going to show the new guest to his room. I waited, tapping my feet intermittently. I made my way back to the reception. Aubrey still hadn't poked her head through the entrance door. I began to wonder if she might have left without me. I'd be stuck at the hotel for the day. The upside of this delay was we might still be at the hotel when Rudi showed up.

"What can I do for you?" Quietly, Alexandre had reappeared with a big smile on his face. He seemed well rested and in a good mood.

"Did he call?"

"Who?" An uncomfortable pause followed. "Rudi?"

"Yes, Rudi! He meant to call the hotel reception if... he... Well, he said he would be here by noon, I think, unless he calls. You see, he... is not here. At least that's what he said." I obviously didn't make the best sense. Alexandre's grin was getting wider by the second.

"You had a date... With Rudi?" Alexandre burst out laughing. It came out of the blue for me. I stared at him, astounded, unable to respond to his unexpected outburst.

"Why are you... laughing at me?" I sounded small and somewhat offended.

"*Pardon, Mademoiselle!* I am not laughing at you. A date just doesn't go with Rudi. It doesn't suit his lifestyle at all." The outburst continued to the point where Alexandre had tears in his eyes. He grabbed a tissue off the table behind the reception and blew his nose hard. The sound resembled a trumpet out of tune, but I was feeling too edgy to find it comical. I took the chance to take another furtive glance at the entrance. It was dim over there. The dark wooden door remained void of motion. "*Mademoiselle Carielle,* make the best of your last day. Go see Paris, the City of Love. It is not worth waiting for Rudi. I am sure he is working today."

"What does he do for a living? Where... does he work?" Alexandre stood rooted to the floor. From one second to another, he had become dead serious.

"No more questions, *Mademoiselle*! Have a good day!"

***

I exited and just about tripped over Aubrey, who was sitting on her backpack on the sidewalk along the hotel's brick wall next to the entrance. She was weeping. Immediately I felt a pang of guilt, which helped me switch gears out of my dilemma. Was Rudi really that important?

"Aubrey! What's going on?" I tried my best tone of voice to sound innocent and clueless at the same time. I bent down to her and put my right hand on her shoulder. She looked up and shot me a glare of raw fury.

"Get your hand off my shoulder! It's all your fault," she hissed.

"What is my fault now?" I gently removed my hand.

"Everything! We were supposed to be staying at the youth hostel, but you messed it up. Our last day is toast because we can't get away from this dump. What's the business between you and the reception? Tell me!" Aubrey used her long-sleeved shirt as a tissue to dry her tears. She shot me another challenging look. "Out with it... Now!"

"Well... I was going to tell you last night but... the tone was... off."

"What tone? We were not playing a duo of clarinet and piano! So what do you mean?" I couldn't believe she was taking this literally. Did she not understand the atmosphere of an environment?

"My goodness, Aubrey! I am talking about the undercurrent of hostility in the room between us. It just didn't feel right to mention..."

"Yes, carry on. I am listening." Aubrey blew her nose. This was my second experience with a trumpeting nose-blowing sound; one for crying, one for laughing.

"Okay, here goes... We had made plans for Rudi to pick us up today and go on a tour together." She instantly interrupted me.

"What do you mean, we? Us? You can certainly take me out of the equation. I was no part of any such arrangement."

"Yes, I mean no. Rudi and I talked about it the other night when I was out here with him. Remember? I came in late with my wet hair in tangles. Really late! Anyway..."

"I was sleeping."

"Oh, yes! To make a long story short, he wanted to stop by here this morning and take us on a tour and then out for dinner."

"You already said that, except for the dinner invitation. Where to? Most definitely not to a fancy restaurant, I am guessing." The dinner idea appeared to please her and cheer her up.

"Anyhow, I didn't want to leave any earlier than eleven. I was hoping he would show up. But he didn't — obviously — and he didn't call. I went inside to confirm with Alexandre that Rudi hadn't called. But I had to wait at the reception. Alexandre is a busy receptionist. We can go now."

"What about dinner?" Aubrey's eyes grew wide.

"What about it? It'll be Free Time or McDonald's at the train station, our usual venues." I heard a note of sadness in my voice. I had no appetite for another cheeseburger with French fries. However, after counting my francs in the morning, I knew I was out of pocket money. I just had enough coins left for an inexpensive meal.

"Right, cheap and unhealthy! A repeat of yesterday and the day before after we pick up our luggage later today."

"Exactly!" I wondered why Aubrey was concerned about an unhealthy meal. "How about another view from the top of Montparnasse Tower?"

"Are you sure you don't want to see Les Invalides or Les Catacombes rather than Montparnasse?" Aubrey sounded less hostile and appeared to want to look at the different options with me for our last hours in Paris.

"Les Invalides is basically a war museum. We already had a touch of war history at L'Arc de Triomphe. Les Catacombes... Skulls under the grounds of Paris. I'd gladly pass unless you want to see them."

"What about Le Centre Pompidou?"

"It's modern art."

"Let's visit Montparnasse Tower then."

"Agreed!"

***

The Métro would never be my favourite means of transportation. The underground stations and tunnels would be barred from sunlight forever. The trains were overcrowded at all times of travel. The smell of humans perspiring knocked me sideways time and again. My eyes were half closed as I listened to the train gliding along on the tracks to Montparnasse district. Aubrey studied the map.

"Montparnasse Tower is an office skyscraper. No museum, no skulls," Aubrey laughed with a genuine expression for the second time since we had arrived. *Maybe she's relieved that we are going home tonight.*

"Meaning there's nothing interesting about it?" I interjected to pick up on her contribution.

"Let's see! It is the tallest skyscraper in France." She quickly scanned the page. "Nothing else other than it was designed by a multitude of French architects with unpronounceable names. Beau... douin. Hoym... How would you say 'Hoym' with a nasal sound? It's just one syllable. And... Campe... non?" Aubrey looked at me flustered in an amusing way. I started laughing from the bottom of my heart. It was just too comical.

"Let me try. Eugène Beaudouin, Urbain Cassan and Louis Hoym de Marien. Montparnasse Tower was eventually built by Campenon Bernard." I giggled.

"It sounds so French when you say it." There was a tone of admiration in Aubrey's voice. My heart skipped a beat. She quickly continued, "Last but not least, it took them four years to construct it, from 1969 until 1973."

"We were in elementary school at that time — eventually..."

"Oops, our station is next. Let's not miss it. It would be a huge waste of time to get off somewhere else and take another Métro back to Montparnasse district while..." Aubrey didn't finish her sentence. We had to get up and move to the line-up at the exit doors. The train stopped. There was an expanding group of people teeming like ants outside the doors. My eyes grew wide, so did Aubrey's. "Move right through them," Aubrey suggested, "I'll meet you at the tail end of this swarming horde. Ready? Let's go!" The Métro doors opened.

"Ready," I said. Clutching my purse, I dove into the crowd. Head tucked down, I burst through the masses. I didn't mean to be rude, but there was no choice but to push through the throng of Métro users. Aubrey had been faster than I. I saw her waiting a few metres down by the underground stairs that would lead us out of the tunnel into the Parisian sunlight. With that awareness I sped up my pace and took a deep breath when I finally reached Aubrey. "How did you get here so quickly?" I was out of breath.

"I took a swing to the left and went around most of the horde. How do you say crowd in French?"

"*Foule.*"

"*Foule?* Sounds like a fool."

"It does." I chuckled. I took a glance up the stairs. We began our ascent to the Montparnasse area.

*****

As we reached the top of the stairs, my eyes fell on two individuals, one sitting, one squatting, along the grey concrete wall opposite the stairs. That wall was only about five metres from where Aubrey and I had stopped. I took a furtive glance at the two men and failed to trust my eyes. Could it be? I stood on the top step now, unable to move an inch. A powerful sensation like a lightning strike went through my body, head to toe. With my feet glued to the stair, I no longer shied away from gazing straight ahead at the sitting man with light brown curls. His face was turned sideways towards the other individual, the squatting one. Their exchange was soft and subdued, their faces revealing friendly intentions. Seconds flew by. Eventually I became aware of Aubrey's presence again. She was beside me, one step lower, looking at them as well. She spoke into my left ear as I was holding my gaze on him.

"Carielle, did you see... Do you see what I see?" I didn't budge. My response was simple.

"Yes! Wait!" I had barely uttered my two-word-reply when I saw the 'squatter' pulling a banknote from his jeans pocket. He placidly dropped it into the black cardboard box that was sitting in front of Rudi's cross-legged position. Rudi immediately thanked him with a broad smile. The 'squatter' got to his feet, greeted Rudi, and took leave. He aimed for the stairs and walked right by us down into the Métro tunnel. When he was out of sight, I gave Aubrey a sign to follow me. I purposely wasn't clear on my intentions since I didn't want her to protest. I walked straight up to Rudi, Aubrey in sync beside me. From close up, there was no more doubt it was him, sitting on the ground begging passersby for francs. He eventually looked up. I started grinning. He wasn't the least bit startled.

"Rudi!" I couldn't think of anything else to say. Any 'hello' would've come out as a stutter.

"Hi," he said, plain and simple. "This is what I do. It pays well." He laughed out loud waving a banknote at us. "I was about to make my way to the hotel. I had to wait for this guy." He held the banknote up high and made it flutter in front of our noses. "Can you smell it? Dinner for three is guaranteed." Rudi laughed louder.

"Well, you would've missed us," Aubrey reminded him. Had she actually talked to him? I couldn't believe my ears. I briefly looked at her face. She kept her eyes on Rudi with an air of empathy.

"Definitely not," Rudi protested. "I called Alexandre. He said you left your bags. I knew you would return to the hotel — eventually. I also know Germans do nothing at the last minute. We'd have ample time for a fancy dinner, accompanied by red wine *à la française*."

"That sounds delicious," Aubrey chimed. "What restaurant will you take us to?"

"Don't worry about dinner yet, Aubrey! We'll find out soon enough!" I interrupted her impoliteness. "Rudi, will you join us for a quick visit to Montparnasse Tower?" Rudi was in the process of collecting his few belongings, dropping his earnings into his jeans pocket. He held on to the banknote and, after a pause of reflection, slid it into his shirt pocket. I was about to ask him whether he really wanted to spend it on dinner with us but thought better of it. He had already made up his mind.

"Sure, I'll come along. It's just a panoramic view of Paris; that's it." The three of us started out in the direction of Montparnasse Tower, Aubrey to the right, I in the middle, Rudi to the left. I couldn't help smiling. Rudi scanned my profile.

"How has Paris been treating you over the last so many days?" He waited.

"Well, let me think," I began to rummage for details...

ELEVEN

AU BON ACCUEIL

The restaurant Rudi took us to was called the *'Au Bon Accueil'*, an upscale bistro with a view of the Eiffel Tower. The dark wooden panels, the burgundy upholstery, and the soft lighting gave emphasis to its cozy, romantic atmosphere. It came across as the most appropriate restaurant for a *rendezvous*. However, it wasn't a *rendezvous* in the original sense, was it? It was a *rendezvous à trois*.

Aubrey and I were lined up behind Rudi at the restaurant door when a host approached us. I felt out of place with my rusty-coloured summer pants and my sky-blue strap top. Aubrey had been wearing the same gear for the entire trip. In addition to that, she had never gone to the trouble of eventually washing her hair. Clearly, the *'Au Bon Accueil'* was too extravagant for us. I stole a glance at

Rudi. He was wearing a patterned dress shirt, his usual style.

"*Table pour trois, s'il vous plaît,*" Rudi declared. The host who greeted us was immaculately dressed, white shirt adorned with a black tie, black vest, black pants, and spotlessly polished black shoes.

"Do you have a reservation, *Monsieur*?"

"Yes, I do. It's under Rudi."

"No last name?" The host looked bewildered, his forehead in wrinkles. Rudi shook his head lightly.

"May I have a moment, please." The host stepped away and disappeared behind a heavy burgundy curtain at the far end of the bistro.

"Rudi," I said with a disconcerted tone in my voice,"I am, I mean, we are not dressed appropriately for this upscale dinner. I am embarrassed. We are embarrassed. I... I mean, we didn't bring outfits to fix ourselves up for this exclusive... chophouse." Rudi smirked at me with a tilt to his head.

"There is no dress code," he laughed, clearly attempting to keep it down, "if... you know the chef." The second part of his reasoning came as a whisper.

"Chef? You know the *chef de cuisine*?" I failed to act surprised as he appeared in front of us.

"Rudi! *Enchanté de te voir!* Nice to see you!" He sounded sincere, then turned to Aubrey and me in a more formal way. "*Mesdemoiselles, enchanté!* I am pleased to receive you at the *'Au Bon Accueil'*. One of the hosts will be getting your table ready momentarily and then take you to your table. Wine is on the house." Aubrey and I instantly exchanged puzzled looks. Both of us obviously hadn't expected this warm but formal reception at the *'Au Bon Accueil'* where no one knew us. I felt even more insecure about my appearance than before when taking another close look at my summer outfit. My eyes landed on my dirty runners that I had been wearing every day for hours of walking.

"Don't worry," Rudi whispered in my ear. "You look stunning. Trust me!" A different host by the name of Jean-Pierre appeared. Rudi took a step away from me. The host turned to Aubrey and me bowing almost imperceptibly.

"*Mesdemoiselles, bienvenue! Suivez-moi, s'il vous plaît.*"

"The French sure know how to top it," Aubrey remarked a little too loud. Fortunately, the chances of Jean-Pierre understanding German appeared slim. The table he took us to in the centre of the restaurant was expertly set and surrounded by three wooden chairs. Jean-Pierre pulled out a chair for me and then for Aubrey. Rudi sat down on the third chair next to me. Jean-Pierre handed out the menus. I held my breath wondering about the dishes and the corresponding prices. I moved closer to the table, opened the menu, and read the names of every dish in detail.

"This chophouse, as you call it, serves elevated meat and seafood dishes," Rudi explained with a grin. He continued cautiously, "I hope you like meat or fish." I realized that the soft conversation was directed at me only. Therefore, I refrained from looking directly at Aubrey. I didn't want to see how excluded she might have felt although she now appeared on better terms with Rudi because he had invited us to this fancy grill. Her change in attitude towards him, though, was unlikely to have anything to do with him personally. I laughed and didn't know why. My eyes fell on the young waiter, clean-cut and spunky, who had appeared out of nowhere with a bottle of red wine.

"*Du Bergerac, Mademoiselle?*" He stepped closer but held a decent distance when he showed me the bottle. I found myself reluctant and indecisive. I looked to Rudi for advice. He nodded.

"*Monsieur,*" I eventually had the courage to address the server with a shaky tone in my voice, "I do not often drink wine. I am not... experienced, to say the least. I looked at Rudi again when I noticed Aubrey had been left out of the wine selection. She just sat there with no input, amused and unaware of what was going on. Her limited French language skills put her on the outside of the conversational cycle. The waiter still stood there like a dummy holding the bottle of *Bergerac*. I couldn't make up my mind and didn't understand why it was up to me to decide on the wine. Eventually, he scurried away and came back with the champagne.

"I'd recommend *Le Bergerac*," Rudi suggested.

"Do you?" I whispered. "Please tell him so because I am fine with either. Unless... you want to ask Aubrey for her opinion."

"*Du Bergerac,*" Rudi announced with a tone of firmness that didn't leave any room for discussion. Had he even heard my suggestion to ask Aubrey as well? The young waiter stood in front of us with the champagne. He turned on his heels and disappeared behind the bar to exchange the champagne for the red wine.

"They sure have much patience with indecisive patrons," I said leaning over to Rudi's chair. I was determined to keep it low, in German or in French. In a flash, the young server reappeared. For the first time I took a glance at his name tag. It said Gaston.

"Just half a glass for me, please, Gaston," I asked with my most polite tone of voice. Rudi frowned at me, then began to chuckle.

"You'll sleep better on the train ride home if you have a full glass." Rudi was getting the giggles. I suddenly perked up.

"*Mademoiselle, du vin rouge?*" Aubrey had been addressed by Gaston. Her eyes were darting back and forth between Gaston, Rudi, and me. Her cheeks looked overly blushed. She began to stutter.

"*Moi... Moi... Moi... Moitié.*" She paused, blushing a little more. I took another sideways glance at Rudi. He smirked and appeared to find it difficult to stay respectfully silent rather than laughing at Aubrey's bumpy attempts to speak French. Then it was his turn, and I looked at him with utmost expectation; so did Aubrey and Gaston from how it seemed.

"I shall have a full glass of this precious *Bergerac*... and more." Gaston hurried around the table to fill Rudi's glass. "Ladies," Rudi lifted his glass towards the centre of the table, "this bottle shall be empty by the end of the night. May you have a safe trip home! Cheers!" Rudi emptied half the glass in one go. My mouth dropped open. Aubrey, on the other hand, was looking at her hands in her lap. I began to feel sorry for her but was left with no time to dwell on it. Why was everyone paying so much attention to me? My attempts to stay inconspicuous were in vain. I was unsure how to behave. Was I meeting the *'Au Bon Accueil's'* expectations?

Gaston was back, notepad and pencil ready, to take our orders. I had only had a fraction of a minute to scan the menu. My tastebuds clearly signalled to me that my appetite was more for fish than meat.

"*Sole De Petits Bateaux De Saint Gilles Croix De Vie,*" I said when Gaston asked me. As before, I was first in line.

"*Bon choix, bon choix,* good choice," Gaston commented in an encouraging way. "One of our best dishes indeed! One of our best fish dishes indeed!" With his chin up, he turned his attention towards Aubrey. Aubrey avoided eye contact with him and addressed me instead.

"Carielle, can you order this for me?" Her dirty index finger had landed on a particular item on the menu. She had pushed the menu over to my placemat.

"Yes, I can," I responded, eager to be able to help her out. "*Monsieur,* Aubrey would like *Pigeon Entier Rôti Et Cuisse Confite, légumes de saison étuvés.*"

"Excellent, excellent," he mumbled to himself without looking at either one of us. "How about yourself, Sir?" Rudi did not have to look at the menu, which made me wonder whether he was a regular guest at this bistro.

"*Côte De Boeuf 'Angus' Grillée, petite salade! Merci, Gaston.*" Rudi folded his menu and handed it to Gaston. Aubrey and I followed suit. We sat together in uncomfortable silence for a short moment as my gut instinct was conveying. How to make conversation with a scientifically-inclined friend from school who had never been away from home on her own, and a German guy whose potentially murky lifestyle was shrouded in mystery and who imaginably lived in Parisian hostels at best? The three of us were an odd trio. Take me out of the equation, and that dinner would've never happened in any circumstance.

All too soon, I no longer had the ability to entertain such thoughts. I was getting tipsy on *Bergerac,* in fact on less than half a glass. I only had wine on special occasions. Maybe this was a special occasion. Soon, in less than three hours, we would be leaving Paris with all its breathtaking views of history and Rudi who, as a German, had chosen a life of some sort in France. A simple question for him came to my mind.

"Why do you live in Paris, Rudi?" My words sounded foreign to me, as if they were coming from faraway places. Gaston, Jean-Pierre, and two other servers hovered around our table for the duration of our dinner at the *'Au Bon Accueil'*. Their true faces appeared hidden behind masks of insincere smiles. Time and again, they held up another bottle of *Bergerac*. I managed to shake my head slightly, hoping they would understand my sign language. I had tasted enough wine for one evening. My head was spinning. Aubrey appeared to me as though she was submerged in ocean waves. The conversation had no meaning and did not make a difference. I was merely enjoying my last evening in Paris giggling and laughing about nothing.

"I didn't like living in bureaucratic Germany," Rudi held his response plain and simple. He didn't sound judgemental. This was the answer, and there didn't seem to be more to it.

With an air of amusement about his face, Rudi kept a close eye on me from his chair. He most likely got a kick out of seeing me tipsy, uninhibited, and, simply put, alive. I was, however, in control of my behaviour. I felt I was revealing a new, rare personality trait of mine while not being so overly serious after having some *Bergerac*. My glass still had a few drops of the red spirit in it. I took another sip, and the waiters seemed to be dancing and singing while rushing to bring our three gourmet dinners besides water, more wine, and espresso. Every bite of my sole dish tasted heavenly. I savoured it slowly and ate with a huge appetite. As far as I could tell, so did Aubrey devouring her duck.

"Better than Free Time?" I asked Aubrey who said very little during dinner. She nodded, forking up her last piece of duck and stuffing it into her mouth. Her etiquette needed much improvement. But we were going home. Her lacking social skills no longer mattered to me. Rudi looked at Aubrey, then at me, and slightly shook his head.

"Excuse me, Carielle!" He pulled a Gauloise from his shirt pocket, got up, and stepped out.

TWELVE

CAMP OUT AND DEPARTURE

Night was beginning to fall when we arrived at the train station in Paris. Aubrey and I were about to board our overnight train through France, Belgium, and Germany back to Brunswick. The spacious Paris train station was surprisingly overcrowded in those evening hours. Travellers with suitcases, roller bags, and backpacks were heading in all directions. The three of us, Rudi included, had to make an effort to stay close to each other, so we wouldn't get separated by hurrying travellers, some of whom were running by us. Something in the atmosphere had changed to a somber touch, and there was a chill in the air around the train station despite the mid-July heat. I somehow didn't feel safe, and therefore my senses went on high alert. My head was achy from too much *Bergerac*, which turned out to be an inconvenience when I felt the need to stay vigilant. In that state of lightheaded discomfort, I looked to Rudi as a guide, who appeared to know Paris inside and out, and who had been caring enough to accompany us on our night of departure. The train would be leaving around eleven. We still had plenty of time to talk about our vacation days in Paris, to reminisce about school, to say goodbye to Rudi, and maybe plan a get-together in the future.

Benches were few and far between, and neither Aubrey nor I felt like venturing too far from our point of departure. After finding a suitable spot along the wall close to our platform, Aubrey and I sat down on our much lighter backpacks for the trip home. Rudi stood in front of me with a serious air about his face. He had turned quiet, in fact alarmingly quiet, for the quick-witted guy that I had become acquainted with. Out-of-the-blue-laughter was one of his specialties that never failed to surprise me, and it was contagious. But there was none of it now.

"What is it?" I asked cautiously. He lowered himself to the floor beside me, his fingertips lightly drumming on his mustache, which I interpreted as a sign of a nervous gesture.

"Well..." he paused. I waited. "It was..." he broke off right there and turned away.

"Are you sad that we are leaving?" I felt there was no reason to beat around the bush. Time was precious, and it was running out. "We could stay in touch?" He finally looked at me with his sad brown eyes.

"Yes, we could," he mumbled, his low-spirited mood clearly audible in his voice.

"Letters? Would you write to me?" Without waiting for his reply, I went backpack diving for a piece of paper, and I was convinced I had a pen somewhere in my purse. Armed with both items, I scribbled my Brunswick address on the piece of paper as neatly as possible while using my knee as a surface. Rudi stole a glance at my writing, shy about it, as he appeared. Once completed, I eagerly handed it to him. He took it, folded it twice, and slid it into his shirt pocket like the banknote he had received from a stranger for our dinner. "Don't lose that piece of paper," I said, sounding as though my life depended on it. Saying nothing else, I handed him my last scrap of paper and my pen. "Now, please, write down your address!" I was beyond impatient to find out where in Paris he lived. Like so many times before, I wondered whether he even had an address. My hands were shaking. Therefore, I tried my best to hide them from his view. With much expectation, I looked at him. I didn't take my eyes off his right hand that was scribbling something on the paper. Would the address be lengthy or just plain short? Which *arrondissement* would he call his home environment? When Rudi was finally done after what felt like endless minutes, he held onto the piece of paper but handed me the pen back. My curiosity rose to a peak. I felt anxious to finally see what he had written down but had to restrain myself from showing signs of jitteriness.

"*Poste restante!*" He stated, clearing his throat. Hesitant, he handed me the scrap of paper with his tiny scribbles. He looked at me, insecure.

"*Poste restante*, general delivery?" I repeated, incredulous. "You don't have a residence of any sort?" I couldn't help but sound frustrated, which was clearly audible in my tone of voice. "*Poste restante?*" I had to ask him again.

"Yes," he affirmed with the magic three-letter-word. I nodded as a sign of understanding and processing.

"Where do you...?"

"Sleep?"

"Yes, and where do you shower?" I felt embarrassed about asking him such a personal question, but it just slipped out of my mouth.

"At the swimming pool."

"At the swimming pool? Any swimming pool?" He laughed out loud at the note of disbelief in my voice.

"There are many swimming pools with clean showers in Paris — obviously."

"Of course," I mumbled. I busied myself putting pen and paper with *poste restante* written on it in my purse. I was unsure of what my face imparted and therefore didn't want to show him my facial expression. Aubrey had been napping with her head leaning against the wall, her legs stretched out, and her buttocks firmly planted on her backpack. She had missed the exchange of my address with him and his *poste restante* with me. I took a glance at my watch.

"We should make our way to the platform. It will soon be time to board the train." Rudi was still sitting in front of me. Our faces were close to one another. He was nibbling on his lower lip while scanning every detail of my eyes and lips. He was near enough to kiss me. A kiss goodbye, maybe? I looked away, double checking my three pieces of luggage. At this unnerving moment of imminent departure, I wasn't about to give in to the possibility of a kiss. Maybe that brief chance came across as an open invitation that I felt reluctant about despite the temptation. Rudi let go and got off the cold floor to lift himself up. He looked at the train at platform six, our platform of departure from Paris according to our tickets. Oddly enough, there were no passengers on platform six at that hour. The train looked deserted.

"Half an hour to go," I said more to myself than to him feeling on the edge. "Aubrey, wake up!" I lightly touched her left arm and shook it. Her face was blushed as on most days. She blinked and rubbed her eyes.

"What? Carielle? Where are we? Are we home yet?" Rudi paid no attention to her. He had his back to us and obviously kept his eyes glued to our train and platform. I wondered why, but not long enough to expand on that thought. Aubrey was still rubbing her eyes.

"We are at the train station in Paris, Aubrey, just about to board the train home. Let's go." She saw Rudi and yawned. In slow motion, she got up, shouldered her backpack, and wiped a tear off her cheek.

"I was fast asleep," she commented.

"Yes, you were," I replied, focusing on Rudi's presence again.

***

We walked to platform six, dragging our luggage, and paused time and again to look around. I followed every potential passenger with my eyes, wondering if they were headed towards platform six and our train. Strangely enough, no one even cast a glance in our direction. It was seven minutes to departure. To be sure, I checked my watch and my train ticket again since my vision was still blurred from half a glass and a few extra sips of *Bergerac*. Rudi kept looking at me with his sad brown eyes. He was unusually quiet and uninvolved, as it were, removed from the setting. As if shrunken in size, he stood small and unmoving except for his fingers twirling his mustache. I was about to say something uplifting to him when I heard it; the sound of a whistle. All three of us instantly looked in the direction of that sound. Briefly becoming aware of the train's smoking chimney, I froze and then came to the realization that the train leaving from a different platform at the far end of the station was most likely ours. If that was the case, how could we not have been aware of it? Was my brain so fogged up that I was unable to locate the right platform? Apart from that, why did I immediately take the blame for this potential mishap? There were three of us obviously not paying attention.

In seconds, the train for Belgium and Germany was out of sight. The only proof of its fading existence was the rumbling on train tracks in the distance. I turned away from all trains, leaving and staying ones, and – all at once sober – spotted the big sign at the entrance to platform six. It was oversized with the word *Arrivées* printed on it, black on white, not easily missed. My mouth fell open.

"I don't believe this!" I blurted out, staring at the sign that clearly marked the arrival section of the train station. For all those hours, we had been waiting in the wrong area, Rudi, Aubrey, and I.

"Carielle, we just missed the train! This is all your fault – again." Aubrey screamed. Her eyes were flashing red. She stared at me with that look of dangerous fury.

"What do you mean, it's all my fault? I am not the only one failing to stumble upon the sign that clearly says we're in the wrong section. How come you didn't see it?" I could've carried on, but I decided against it.

"You're the one who speaks French!" She claimed with the volume on her voice turned up. Passengers were beginning to turn around and glare at us. I ignored them.

"You mean you're not capable of understanding the French word for arrivals?"

"I was sleeping!"

"That's not an excuse. My head was spinning. That's not an excuse, either."

"What about Rudi?"

"Leave him out of it. He has nothing to do with our trip. It was a nice gesture of his to accompany us to the station. He's under no obligation to manage our departure."

"Of course you would say that. Defending him. Defending the drifter!" Aubrey had a wild look of despair about her and started to sob. She covered her face with her hands as though she meant to hide her rolling crocodile tears from us.

"You missed the train. You'll take the next one." Rudi sounded all logical about it. "No reason to get worked up over it." It appeared simple enough.

"So? What if our train tickets are not valid for the next ride? We have no money. I have four francs left." Aubrey dug for the coins in her jacket pocket and threw them on the ground. "This much won't even buy me a meal." Rudi and I looked at each other. I felt helpless. The scientist was not carved out for street adventures. Aubrey turned away from us, walked a few steps, took her backpack off her shoulders, and tossed it on the ground with a loud thud. She sat down on it. *Déjà vu!*

"We'll have to find out when the next train leaves tomorrow. Can you help me find the ticket counter, Rudi?" I hoped he would hang around for a bit.

"Sure thing," he said. "I know where it is."

"Also, we'll have to spend the remainder of the night at the station because... Well, we have no more travel money to book another night at the hotel." I was somewhat embarrassed about this revelation.

"You can't stay here." Rudi stated matter-of-factly.

"We can't? Why not?" I was astounded.

"Because... No one is allowed overnight at the train station in Paris. It closes at one in the morning. You... I mean we will have to leave and find an... alternative." He looked at me with eyes flickering new light. I took a sideways glance at Aubrey. She was still sitting on her backpack without taking action of any sort. Her head was buried in her hands.

"Not made for travel," Rudi judged with extreme seriousness.

"Should I be worried?" I asked him.

"Just don't travel with her again. She's not made for time away from home. Not at this stage, anyway."

"What's your idea for... the night? You said we can't stay here. Where can we go and... be safe?" I had to admit to myself I felt apprehensive about spending a night in the open air of Paris. Rudi grinned and grinned. It almost sent a shudder down my spine. He was back to his usual comical self, which made me feel safer in an uncomfortable situation away from home.

"Let's go to the ticket counter. Then I'll tell you. Will your friend tag along with us?" He made a face. I burst out laughing. Then I tried to copy it. "The look on your face is hilarious," he said soberly. Aubrey turned around.

"What's so funny?" She sounded stubborn and appeared to be stewing. I walked up to her.

"Rudi and I will be trying to find a ticket agent. Would you like to come with us or stay behind?"

"I'll come." Aubrey was up on her feet in a heartbeat. My guess was she did not want to be left behind fretting about her current situation. She didn't bother shouldering her backpack. She was a few steps behind us dragging her pack along on the ground. At that moment, I could picture her as a mulish toddler dragging her doll. It looked out of place at her age, especially with that sulking look on her face.

To my surprise, the ticket counter was still open.

"You go," Rudi said. "I'll wait out here." He nodded encouragement. Aubrey walked by him and waltzed into the ticket office ahead of me. She stood in front of the ticket counter shrugging her shoulders when the elderly gentleman working the counter addressed her with a question, obviously in French.

"Carielle, get in here," she commanded through the door. I closed my eyes for a moment to be still. Then I turned on my heels and walked in. The elderly gentleman looked at me over the top of his glasses.

"What can I do for you?" He put down a piece of paper that he was holding in his hands and approached the counter.

"*Bonsoir, Monsieur!* Good evening, Sir. We missed our train tonight. Can we get on the next train with our existing tickets?" I held my breath as he took my ticket, pushed his glasses up, and read the information.

"Yes, you can use your ticket as long as it hasn't been stamped. There were some last-minute changes in regards to the platform of departure." Hearing that I breathed a sigh of relief. Aubrey then handed over her ticket as well.

"That is great news," I exclaimed. "When is the next train going via Brunswick in Germany?" The ticket agent took a few steps over to a large timetable on the wall. Again, I held my breath. I was hoping it would be the next morning, and not late at night, since we had no more money to buy food.

"Via Brunswick? Yes! There is a train leaving here from platform seven at 08:23 a.m. Be here at least thirty minutes early. I can assign you new seats now. That way, there will be no need for you to stop by the ticket counter tomorrow morning when it's busy." The ticket agent looked at me again over the top of his glasses. Was he wondering what had happened? He took a glance at Rudi through the glass door, then went to work assigning Aubrey and me new seats. "The lad out there is not travelling?" He asked while writing on our tickets. I was right. He was wondering.

"No, he's not," I stammered and left it at that.

"I didn't think so. He looks familiar to me." He took another peculiar glance at Rudi through the glass door as if he were in the wanted files while handing me the tickets with the corrected seat numbers. "Don't miss that train," he warned in a comical way. "Now get out of the train station. They will close the iron gates very soon."

"*Merci, Monsieur!* Thank you, Sir." I handed Aubrey her ticket as I made my way through the door. *Why would Rudi look familiar to the ticket agent?*

The three of us stood at a loss of some sort scanning each other's faces. Did none of us want to break the silence? We heard a click. In unison, we turned around to witness the ticket agent locking the door to the ticket office. He gave us a sign to leave. I nodded his way. Eventually Rudi spoke.

"We'll take the exit that will lead us to the Métro station. There's the 01:00 a.m. train that will take us to a safe spot to spend the night."

"Where to?" Aubrey interrupted.

"Let me finish," Rudi's voice struck a chord of impatience. He continued under his breath. "It might be risky. There's... questionable folks hanging out between the train station and the Métro station. I'll be walking between you two. Aubrey, lock arms with me on the left. Carielle, lock arms with me on the right. Now! Let's go before they lock us in." Both Aubrey and I stared at Rudi. I was stunned.

"Wouldn't it be safer to get locked in?" I felt my question had validity. Rudi chortled.

"If you get caught, you'll pay a steep fine. I definitely don't need it. Neither do you girls." He paused briefly as the high ceiling lights dimmed row by row. "There's no more time to toss around options. Let's go!" As Rudi had instructed, we locked arms with him. "Clutch your purses! Make them invisible!" As best as we could, we concealed our purses from view. Rudi and I began walking leg to leg, hip to hip, shoulder to shoulder. I wondered how Aubrey felt doing the same on his other side. She would be uncomfortable, I knew that much. I was having mixed feelings about it. I enjoyed it but at the same time didn't want to allow myself that sensation.

We walked at a quick pace but did not run. The tunnel was darkish with lights emitting an eerie glow of amber. There were passageways going off the main tunnel. I did not have the courage to look down those passageways, afraid someone or something might jump out at us. Nonetheless, the walk to the Métro station was short. We made it through the tunnel without an incident; without being seen by any of those... questionable folks, as Rudi had called them. As we neared the Métro station, Rudi let go of my arm and of Aubrey's; then he breathed a sigh of relief. Needless to say, I had so many questions for him — again — but did not want to ask, especially after he had looked rather troubled on the tunnel walk.

A light wind was blowing. I welcomed the cooled down summer air moving about me. What would happen next? We were obviously waiting for the last Métro. It was fifty minutes past the hour of midnight. Some distance away, I saw a young girl with long blond hair waiting by herself on the platform. She was dressed in a white windbreaker jacket. On second glance, she looked like a high school girl with a knapsack full of books. I, on my part, would not have been brave enough to hang out by myself at the Métro station at that hour of night. I would have considered it foolish. I was uneasy enough as it was, despite the three of us being together. My next look landed on Aubrey. She appeared terrified as in most unusual occurrences. Therefore, it concerned me less and less. I was, however, hoping she would not pass out on us. Rudi who was staring into the distance lit a cigarette with a slight tremble of his hands. While I disliked the smell of the strong Gauloises, I enjoyed being surrounded by the smoke he puffed into the air when exhaling deeply. It told me he hadn't left us because he obviously cared enough to be around.

"Carielle, take me to a phone! I need to call my parents!" Aubrey's voice was tinged with terror. Her face had gone from pale to white. Her ice-cold fingers closing around my lower left arm felt like the clammy grip of death. Her eyes were about to fall out of their sockets as she pleaded with me. Rudi came rushing to the scene and stopped beside Aubrey. He gently took my left arm and pulled it out of her deadly grip.

"Let go," he instructed Aubrey. "Let go!" His voice grew in volume. She hesitated.

"Aubrey, you may call your parents if you find a phone booth, but what would it do? Think about it! They'd be up all night worrying about you, at the same time being unable to do anything at all for your safety so far away from home." I caught my breath for emphasis. "They'd be worried sick about you spending the night in Paris without accommodation. Is that what you want?" There was no answer out of her. When she finally opened her mouth, a squeak of a tone came out. What then followed out of her was drowned out by the roaring sound of the last Métro pulling into the station. I turned with unfounded expectations. The compartments were brightly lit. Not surprising, though, but somewhat troubling, there was no one on the train. The train stopped, and instantly the doors flew open as if set in motion by invisible hands. I felt a shudder zigzagging down my back. Rudi shot me a quick look as if he wanted to be assured that I was fine. Rushed as he seemed, he took quick steps towards the open Métro doors, and I hurried right behind him with an almost uncontrollable urge to hold on to him. Aubrey trailed behind us, not appearing any more appeased than before my short lecture. Rudi sat down on a bench that could easily have seated three passengers, and I slid in beside him. Aubrey chose the same row across the aisle but sat by herself. The girl with the fair complexion from the platform sat down a few benches ahead of us, took out a fair-sized volume of a book, and started reading. She appeared as though it was the most natural thing in the world for her as a school-girl to be out and about in Paris at night. The only other passenger on the last Métro was a drunkard a few rows back.

"How far are we going?" I talked quietly, being mindful of Aubrey who might have ended up with another panic attack if she had heard too much about the way we'd be spending the night. Rudi yawned.

"Let's say a few stations." Vague sounded just like him. I nodded, and my mind, still somewhat foggy, trailed off to our first afternoon in Paris when we met Rudi at the youth hostel.

"Why did you help us?" I whispered.

"When? Now?" Rudi looked mystified.

"Right from the start!"

"You are a village beauty in need to be rescued." He began to snicker.

"That's the reason?"

"Yeah, more or less!"

"Well, I am not from a village. Brunswick is a fairly big city." We looked at each other and began to giggle. In no time, we had reached the second stop, and the long-haired girl whose face I never had a chance to clearly see, got up and got off. She walked into the dimly lit, deserted Métro station by herself. It gave me the creeps.

"This is not unusual," Rudi said following my gaze.

"What is not unusual?"

"Girls being out at night."

"Isn't it dangerous?"

"Next stop is ours. Wake your friend." Aubrey's head was hanging down and rolling back and forth between her shoulders.

"Despite her fear, she sure sleeps a lot," I commented to Rudi. "Aubrey, wake up, please!" Aubrey moaned and opened her eyes. "Get up," I instructed. "Our station is next."

The Métro doors burst open, and we quickly stepped out and into the night. The night resembled an ink pot of sheer black. Rudi walked ahead with a quick pace. I followed close behind. Aubrey slowed us down by dawdling with an obvious unwillingness to move forward. Rudi was visibly agitated about having to frequently stop and turn around. With me being stuck walking between the two, I felt like a mother dealing with an impatient husband in front of me and a stubborn child behind me. It was a painful journey towards an unknown destination.

"It's down there." Rudi stopped abruptly, pointing with his right index finger towards a spot under an overpass. I looked and looked but was unable to clearly sketch out the structure of the location.

"What's down there?" Aubrey asked with a curious tone of voice. Rudi had already moved on. For that reason, Aubrey's question remained unanswered. I was so focused on staying close behind that I didn't want to waste any time on explanations. We had reached a bank of piled-up gravel.

"Take small steps down, or slide down on your rear ends," Rudi suggested. It was a relief to see him smile again on this starless night. Already halfway down the gravel bank, he stretched out his left hand towards me. I was about to take small steps on the gravel when I realized I'd be sliding down on my soles if I didn't take his offer. I grabbed his hand and tightly held on to it while making my way down. Aubrey still stood at the top watching. Would she want his assistance or decide to slide down?

Rudi and I had just reached the bottom when we witnessed a landslide of gravel rushing towards us. Aubrey, barely visible in the dust cloud she was causing, came sledding down on her backpack. She stopped short next to my feet. I couldn't help but giggle. She was a hilarious sight, all covered in dust. When she peeled her backpack off the ground, she realized that it now had several holes in it. *Oh my!* I was so glad it was too dark for her to see the gigantic grin on my face.

"It'll be fine, Aubrey, until we get home." Looking at her, I thought it wise to appease her rather than waiting for another uncontrollable outburst of various emotions. Rudi cautiously approached our spot under the overpass.

"Here's where we'll stay until about 05:00 a.m. Let me find some cardboard boxes. I'll be right back." Rudi was out of sight in an instant. Aubrey and I stood glued to the spot waiting for him to return.

"Have you noticed...?" Aubrey whispered flashing her pocket-knife.

"Noticed what? You don't need that." I reminded her by pointing at the blade. But she kept the knife sticking straight out in front of her.

"There's someone sleeping along the wall a few steps from us." I strained my eyes to make out a figure. But all I saw with my squinting was an accumulation of cardboard boxes.

"He's hiding inside the boxes, snoring lightly." Aubrey sounded clever.

"Don't worry about the *clochard*," Rudi said, returning from his search. "He's drunk and out. He is no harm to anyone!" Rudi began to take the cardboard boxes apart that he had brought back. He spread them out on the ground next to a post that would hide us from immediate view.

"There you go. This will serve as a mattress for better comfort." With a glow of expectation in his eyes, he obviously waited for a comment from us on this genius idea. Aubrey and I both had nothing to add. "Well, it'll do. I don't have blankets." He sounded deflated. Aubrey and I took a step closer to Rudi's creation of a camping spot. I stared at the wavy cardboard, and in slow motion, I put my backpack beside it and lowered myself to the ground. When sitting, I took a good look around me.

"Rudi, what's close to here?" I looked up at him in the dark. It was impossible to make out his facial features. Our camp-out-spot felt deserted and far from touristic Paris. Strangely enough, Laura Branigan's song 'Self Control' kept going through my mind. It was a big hit in Europe at the time that had accompanied me throughout the trip. Maybe I had even heard it play from one of the bars on the way to our current location. Quietly I was humming to myself. Eventually, we had all found a seat on the cardboard, waiting for nothing to happen. Aubrey sat back-to-back with me. Rudi sat across from me. He finally answered.

"Le Centre Pompidou is a short walking distance from here."

"Guess what," I said embarrassed, "before we all lie down and go to sleep, I'll have to pee, and it's urgent. I am about to explode. Can you take me to a restroom of some sort? I am not picky." I had talked fast to get it off my chest. There was a pause of uncomfortable silence. Was he about to roll his eyes asking me why I didn't say anything earlier?

"How far can you walk?" He wanted to know.

"Not far!" I was desperate. Aubrey was already in her horizontal position, covered up with her summer jacket. I saw the blade of her pocket-knife blink against a streetlight. I got up. The sight of us would've made me laugh if my physiological need hadn't been unbearable. Rudi and I both looked at Aubrey.

"Hey, Aubrey," I said, "do you want to come with us?" She shook her head and pulled her summer jacket all the way up to her chin. She closed her eyes as though she no longer wished to be addressed by us.

"Let's go, then!" Rudi put his left arm around my waist and pulled me towards him. Then he switched sides and took my left hand into his right. He led the way up the gravel mountain. Holding on to him, I followed with tiny steps. I caught my breath once we had made it up to the sidewalk.

"I thought they say Paris never sleeps. The city looks asleep to me now." I tried to distract myself from my discomfort.

"Depends on where you are. It is never busy in this area. Tourists have no reason to come here."

"How far is it, Rudi? I am so uncomfortable."

"Look up ahead. It's the backside of Le Centre Pompidou. We're going there because, well, I imagine you would appreciate some privacy. The backside has enormous posts like the biggest tree trunks you have ever seen. You can hide behind one and find relief." He looked genuinely concerned. "I'll stay close by, behind the next post if you like, so I can always come to your rescue in case someone decides to creep up on you."

"*Clochards?*" I must've sounded ridiculous because Rudi started laughing into the night. "Hey," I said, "you are waking the dead and attracting who knows whom..." That made him laugh even louder. I felt exposed and stopped to look around me. There was no one, just the silent surroundings temporarily eclipsed by the light. Rudi kept leading the way, pulling me along. My hand was loosely hanging on to his. I was in too much pain to pinpoint the sensation of us walking hand in hand. Then, out of the blue, the enormous posts appeared. I breathed a sigh of relief. We had arrived at the backside of Le Centre Pompidou.

"Look," he pointed to the next post with his right index finger after letting go of my hand. "I'll be waiting behind that one. I promise I will not look over here. Come to that post when you're done." Rudi didn't bother waiting for my response. He immediately left for the next post that was approximately ten metres away. After he had vanished, I took care of my physiological business with light speed. I saw a puddle, then a flood.

"Oh, my goodness," I whispered into the night after taking a glance at the creek I had created. Keeping my safety in mind, I hurried and then made my way over to Rudi's post as swiftly as I could.

"You just flooded Paris," he grinned while taking my hand as before.

"I feel so much better. Thank you, Rudi!" I planted a soft kiss on his cheek. He smiled looking at the ground in front of us.

Aubrey was still in the same position when we returned. Her pocket-knife was loosely sitting in her right hand next to her face. The blade was hidden.

"That took a long time! Did you guys travel on foot to the other end of town?" Her remark came through a hoarse voice and sounded more like a complaint and in no need of a response. Without even a moment's contemplation, I went to lie down next to Aubrey. Then Rudi lowered himself down to get comfortable beside me. I was sandwiched between the two. Rudi and I were finally settled on the cardboard, facing each other but not touching.

"Would you mind spreading out my summer jacket, so it covers me a bit better?" I asked him politely, smiling away. He jumped up and did a meticulous tucking in, as a dad would do saying good night to his daughter. "You don't have a jacket, Rudi?"

"I don't need one in this heat." It was obvious.

"But it cools off at night. Can't you feel it?"

"No! I feel anything but cooled off right now." He settled down on the cardboard again.

"Rudi, where do you sleep when you don't take girls in distress to this location?" I waited, my eyes getting heavy. He could've chuckled but he didn't. "And one more thing,"

I yawned, "were you aware that we would miss the train?" There was nothing but the sound of night, and Rudi for a moment appeared translucent like a ghost when I drifted off to sleep a moment later.

***

Eventually I woke up. It was still dark, which meant I hadn't slept long. It took me a split second to figure out where I was and with whom. To my surprise, Rudi's left hand was planted on my waist and the back of his right on my abdomen. My right knee had slipped between his legs... — I made no sound and didn't move. Instead, I listened to Aubrey and Rudi's breathing. Aubrey was deeply snoring, which left no doubt she was fast asleep. Rudi's breathing was short and shallow. Was he asleep or just pretending to be? I put my right hand on his left arm to see whether he'd move his hand off my waist. He firmed up his grip and lightly squeezed my skin. At this point, I knew he was awake. He opened his eyes. His face was only an inch from mine. We looked into each other's eyes until we teared up. Neither of us spoke. Rudi pulled me closer to him. I didn't pull back. Was I ready for this emerging intimacy right before my departure from Paris? The situation didn't allow me to entertain such thoughts. Rudi pressed his lips to mine. We began to kiss tenderly at first until the kisses became more urgent in nature and more penetrating. I began to feel liquid and out of breath.

"Rudi, please!" I whispered. "I need to catch my breath!" I swallowed. "Also...!"

"Also, what?" He mumbled.

"Well, I am... unsure about this... closeness."

"You are spoiling the moment, Carielle! I thought you liked me."

"I do like you. In all honesty I do!" I felt shy and didn't know what else to say. "I have to admit... I am... just... uncomfortable right now and right here." I cast a quick glance at Aubrey even though I was convinced she wasn't the only inconvenience to our emerging intimacy. My eyes moved ahead to the wall. The *clochard* sighed in his sleep and suddenly — with obvious effort — moved onto his other side. His face was now visible to us. It was a weather worn face with reddish leathery skin. A shudder went through me. I began to shiver. Rudi put my summer jacket around my shoulders.

"Let's lie down again. I promise I won't do anything that might make you feel uncomfortable." There was a pause of indecision on my end. But I was too drained to argue against his suggestion. Once settled, I put my head against Rudi's chest and closed my eyes. His heartbeat calmed me down. But not for long... There was a dark figure of a man popping up out of nowhere. His dark complexion and slick black hair matched his ochre suit. He quickly approached the post that covered us from view. About to relieve himself, he spotted the three of us lying on the ground. He gasped.

"Not here!" Rudi sounded like a commander. "Please!" He emphasized our obvious need for an unsoiled site. The dark figure made no attempt to argue. He instantly ran off without looking back. Rudi breathed a sigh of relief and whistled. "Close call! The guy likely thinks we are in the middle of a threesome." Rudi clearly didn't appear embarrassed about stating the facts. It sounded so normal business the way he said it. I frowned and grinned at the same time. I was in fact beginning to feel concerned about our safety. Was our camp-out-site really secluded enough for some undisturbed rest?

"What about the *clochard*, Rudi? What if he wakes up and sees us?"

"He's unlikely to know what's happening around him. You do not need to worry!" Rudi sounded as though he no longer wished to talk about the *clochard*. Then he made a startling statement. "He is who I am." The revelation lingered in the air around us as Rudi went silent and appeared reflective.

"There's no history to you? You are just a *clochard*?"

"My history has taken me to where I am now."

"I would like to know who I am kissing. To some extent..." Maybe this wasn't funny, but I couldn't help but giggle.

"Suffice it to say, I will tell you later."

"Later ends in a few hours."

"You gave me your address. I will come visit and enlighten you."

"When?"

"As soon as we can arrange it." I felt defeated and quickly curled up on the cardboard, turning around towards Aubrey. I put my right arm under my head for support.

"You are ever more vague," I said looking up at him. He was now sitting motionless on the cardboard, his curly dark blond hair sticking out like sun rays against the starless sky.

"I've learned to be cautious. It's part of my *métier*."

"I imagine you will enlighten me about your *métier* at a later time, too." I tried not to sound disappointed. I checked my watch. It was ten to four. I closed my eyes and heard the familiar sound of a Gauloise coming out of a pack of cigarettes. Rudi got up, lit his Gauloise, and disappeared from view.

***

A few minutes after five in the morning, we solemnly walked towards Montmartre and Le Sacré Cœur. The appearance of this stunning white cathedral was surreal at this time of dawn. Rudi, Aubrey, and I remained silent while taking in its splendour. Eventually Rudi stopped, turned towards us, and gave us each a franc.

"There's a musical bathroom up ahead. Put your coin in, and you'll have five minutes to freshen up with some chill-out music playing in the background. The door will open automatically. You'll have to be off the can within five minutes." Aubrey and I nodded in unison while I was trying to stifle a laugh. The word 'can' for toilet wasn't a word widely used in my hometown.

"You go first," I said to Aubrey.

"No, you can go first," she responded to me.

"Okay then!" I wasn't going to argue with her again. We had done enough bickering during our time together in Paris. I stepped up to the bathroom and put my franc into the slot next to the bathroom door. It swung open immediately. I went inside, and the door swung shut. I took a quick look around this modern contraption. It was spacious and gave the user the impression of being inside a globe. It even had a shower. *Who in this world can shower in five minutes?* Then my eyes fell on the door mechanism. I realized that there was a slot for coins on the inside of the door. The user would have to keep feeding the coin slot for the door to stay closed and locked. In a flash, I used the can, as Rudi had called it, and freshened up at the sink. I brushed my hair, but there was no time to touch up my make-up. The bathroom door swung open just as I finished. I walked out. Aubrey hurried to the bathroom door with a quick step to put her franc in the slot when Rudi interrupted her.

"Give it five minutes. The bathroom door won't open until the cleaning cycle is done. After each use, the bathroom gets hosed down." We stood and waited.

Eventually, Aubrey took her turn and disappeared inside the globe. Here was another chance for me to talk to Rudi in private for five minutes. But I was struggling to find the right words and the appropriate tone on an adventurous morning after a sleepless night out in the open. Therefore, I decided to stay silent with a glare into the distance. Rudi stood a few metres away about to light another Gauloise. He began to pace back and forth taking long drags from his cigarette. By the time Aubrey reappeared, he had flicked the butt across the sidewalk into the hedges. "The Métro station is up ahead," he said matter-of-factly.

***

The train was already waiting. I was anxious to get on. Rudi, Aubrey, and I crowded around the access point.

"Let's go," Aubrey said, completely ignoring Rudi's presence. "I don't want a repeat of last night." Aubrey shouldered her backpack and approached the access point. Slowly, as if to think about it, she turned around to take another glance at Rudi. "Bye, Rudi! Thanks for dinner. Carielle, I'll be on the train. See you shortly." She left in a hurry with much determination in her step. Rudi said nothing in return. He was dead silent. I had already learned that he didn't fancy goodbye scenarios. He appeared insecure about what to say.

"Well, Rudi, this sums it up. I am indebted to you for all the time you've spent assisting us on this unusual trip. I will never forget your kindness. Thank you with all my heart!" I planted a kiss on his forehead. He stood motionless looking past me. "Please say something!" I waited two minutes, three minutes... "Well?"

"Send me a letter as soon as you can! *Poste restante*!" At last, a few words out of him rang like music in my ear.

"*Poste restante* it is!" I tried a vague smile. Now it was my turn to shoulder my backpack.

"When do you think I can visit?" It sounded urgent.

"September before school might work. I'll be moving to a different town, not too far from Brunswick."

"When?"

"Haven't planned that far ahead. Visit me at home! My parents have a bedroom for guests set up in the attic. Staying up there is heavenly. Bye now!"

"*Poste restante!*"

"You don't need to keep reminding me." While saying it with a smile, I went through my purse and found the piece of paper that he had scribbled on the night before. I waved the note through the air in front of my face for him to see. "*Poste restante...* I'll put this in my backpack pocket right now and zip it up. Bye, now!" I turned towards the train and started walking, slowly but steadily. Just as I took the steps to board the train, I turned around towards the access point. Rudi was gone.

***

The train ride home was uneventful. This time, I had a window seat, and Aubrey was stuck in a middle seat across from me, visibly spilling over the armrests. I did not feel like talking and therefore refrained from looking her way. Due to the lack of interaction, no one in the same compartment would've guessed that we were acquainted and travelling together. I watched the landscape zoom by in France, Belgium and finally Germany. At major train stations where we stopped for more than thirty minutes, I watched passengers get on and off and wondered where their stories would take them and for how long. I remembered travelling on the train as a little girl with my grandmother when we went to visit relatives across the border in East Germany. Train rides were exciting adventures back then, and they also easily rocked me to sleep. Those early years of my young life felt like an eternity gone by.

THIRTEEN

RUDI'S VISIT

Aubrey's goodbye at our arrival station in Brunswick had been frosty. A potential get-together for the purpose of exchanging photos was talked about on vague terms. She appeared happy to get away from me, and most importantly, to get home to her family, whom she had not called from Paris.

After unloading my travel gear and getting a good night's sleep, I set out to write my first letter to Rudi, *poste restante* in Paris...

***

Rudi arrived in early September. I was unsure what to expect, hoping he wouldn't have unreasonable expectations of me in terms of expanding our relationship into something more. I now had a boyfriend, a church organ player who had been introduced to me by a mutual friend. It was still an unsteady connection, and, young as I was, I felt in doubt about so many aspects of that budding relationship. My feelings for him, his commitment to me, our compatibility were all issues up in the air. As much as I tried to get my finger on some of it, the issue I contemplated would evade me, leaving the same trail of unsteadiness. His name was Gert.

"When is he coming?"

"Any time today!" I responded casually. My mother had asked me this same question several times. "I am not comfortable with him staying in the house."

"Why not?" I was — in fact — not interested in her reasons for her discomfort about Rudi staying for a short little while.

"Aubrey told me about him on the phone, the drifter, as she nicknamed him. She said she constantly felt in danger in his presence." I burst out laughing.

"Mom, he was helping us. If it wasn't for him, who knows where we would've ended up. I, on the other hand, was very comfortable in his presence."

"That's because your sense of judgement was off. You're not using your brain wisely, especially around a tramp like him. You even invited him to visit us." She left the kitchen and disappeared into the staircase to make her way up to the attic. I shook my head, finished my cup of tea, went to the door, opened it, and called out into the staircase.

"Why does Aubrey's judgement matter? Why do you attach importance to what Aubrey says? Don't you trust me?" I waited. She rumbled down the stairs.

"Watch your mouth!" She hissed, passed by, and left me standing in limbo. Right at that moment of an evolving issue, the doorbell rang. I stood stock still. My heart began to thump louder in my chest. I could feel its beat in my throat.

"I'll get it," I said to my mother in a normal tone of voice. I took two steps at a time, zoomed by my grandmother's apartment door, and flew to the main entrance of the house. With a heavily thumping heart, I opened the door. "Rudi!" I exclaimed, sounding his name out with special emphasis and a touch of music. I had to restrain myself from falling into his arms. He grinned.

"You look the same, big dark blond curls, a striped shirt *à la* Rudi." I was out of breath. "Come in. It's a bit of a climb up to the attic."

"This is where you live? An apartment house in Brunswick? It looks very well-kept for its age." Rudi took a glance around.

"Yes, my parents have done a lot of work on it. On the yard, too! My grandmother lives on the ground floor, right here." I pointed towards her door six steps up from where Rudi and I were standing. "My parents are one flight up. My sister and I share a living space of two bedrooms and a bathroom upstairs, right under the attic. There's another small apartment next door to us for renters."

"Sounds wealthy," he joked. "Does Aubreyeyey live here, too?" Now it was my turn to start grinning.

"Of course not!"

"Ah! I am getting my hopes up." Rudi sounded optimistic, and I chose to ignore this last comment of his, whatever he was referring to.

"Let me introduce you to my mom before we climb up to the attic." I began to feel apprehensive. Immediately, I had the feeling that Rudi was able to sense my tension. I opened the door to my parents' apartment. "Mom? Mom?" I hesitated and tried again. "Mom?" There was no sound. I could've heard a pin drop. "Sorry, Rudi, she may be... occupied somewhere else in the house or is visiting with my grandma. We'll try to catch her later. Let's go up. By the way, where's your luggage?"

"Just this... A small knapsack." He turned around to show me the pack he was carrying on his back. "It holds everything I need."

"Rudi, by the way, how did you get here?" It instantly appeared he was caught off-guard by this question, and just looked at me, and said nothing. I waited in silence. We were both standing at the bottom of the ladder to the attic in a staring contest. Eventually, I decided to end the game. "I imagine you will enlighten me about it later." He nodded with a smile. I climbed up the ladder ahead of him. He followed me. "The ceiling is low. Please watch your head!" Rudi stepped up and took a look around. His eyes fell on the mattress adorned with taupe coloured bedding. There was a small closet next to the mattress. There was a bench no higher than a low coffee table. The window offered the guest an excellent view of the sky. "Do you like it?" Maybe my question was too direct.

"That's an understatement. I love it," he affirmed, his face shining a little brighter. "I won't be staying long, though." His voice switched to a somber note without transition.

"How so?" I was incredulous.

"Business..." He took a step towards the window, looked out, and ignored my nonverbal response to his answer.

"Well, Rudi, make yourself at home. I have plans to go out tonight. Would you care for a light supper of grilled cheese sandwiches and raw vegetables?"

"Oh, yay, I'd like that very much. Thank you!"

"I'll prepare some for us, and we can eat up here. By the way, you can use the bathroom on the landing at the bottom of the ladder. I'll be back soon." I climbed down and took the staircase to the next lower floor, to my parents' apartment. I found my mom in the kitchen, ignoring me. "Mom, I was going to introduce you to Rudi."

"Yes. It can wait until tomorrow." I had no words for her response and busied myself preparing sandwiches. I boiled water for tea and made another trip up the ladder to find out if Rudi wanted pop, juice, or water to drink. I also kept an eye on the time since Gert was going to pick me up at six.

Rudi and I were both sitting cross-legged on the carpeted floor in the attic, chewing on delicious grilled cheese sandwiches. He broke the silence first.

"These are so tasty. Are you a good all-around cook?"

"No. I don't spend much time in the kitchen. I am not a fan of the kitchen. I did this for you... for us." The sunlight was slowly waning and now shining in at a specific angle, which set the entire attic aglow.

"The light in here... It's exceptional. I have never noticed it. I don't spend time in the attic." I took a glance around, and Rudi took a sip of his lemonade. He just nodded. I checked my watch. "Gert is picking me up in forty minutes. I'll run the dishes down to the kitchen. Then I'll... have to get ready to go. Is there anything else I can delight you with?"

"Your presence," Rudi said dryly.

"I meant in terms of food...!"

"I am good, Carielle. I will see you when you get home."

"Oh, it'll be late, later. You'll be sleeping." Rudi burst out laughing.

"It's good to know you are all up to date about my sleep cycle." We both chuckled.

"Then you must be a night owl like me...!" I said, making my way down the ladder while juggling dinner plates.

***

"Boy, you are late!" Rudi's face showed at the top of the ladder. He looked like a prophet with a halo. The opening to the attic was rectangular from my point of view. So Rudi appeared portrayed in a rectangular frame.

"Hi!" I replied and looked towards my room door. "I would like to get ready for bed. Will see you in the morning." I took a step towards my door and put my left hand on the handle, about to open it.

"Carielle, how was your evening? Come up and tell me. Ten minutes!" There was no hesitation on my end. I had no willpower to resist his invitation and climbed up the ladder at snail speed, so I wouldn't wake my parents. Once up, I dropped my purse and my fall jacket on the floor right on top of Rudi's scattered items. I sat down across from him.

"I shouldn't be going out while having a guest over. I apologize." I sounded more tired than I felt. "The date was planned before you arrived."

"Did you kiss him? Do you love him?" Rudi stared at me.

"What?" I was buying time.

"You heard me. Do you love him?"

"Well... I just started going out with him in August. We're still getting to know each other. Love is not the right way of putting it... yet."

"If I may ask, what attracts you to him?"

"For the most part, he's good-looking with curly dark brown hair and green eyes. He plays the organ in a church on the outskirts of Brunswick. It sounds spectacular. I used to play the flute in a marching band. Music is a common interest."

"Did you meet him at the church?"

"Yes. I joined a mutual friend on Sundays for their service and also for a special church event where I got to know Gert better."

"You still going?"

"No. Hilke, the mutual friend, moved out of town to study theology."

"Oh, I understand, she dragged you into it." Rudi rolled his eyes.

"I needed some stability. Joining her gave me that stability. I am ready to carry on with my own life now."

"Is he religious, too?"

"Not like Hilke. But to some extent, I would say so!"

"Is he a good lover?" I looked at Rudi with an air of disbelief and embarrassment.

"You are lacking social refinement, Rudi. Let's talk about you for once! Or my time's up."

"I am jealous." The silence that followed was unbearable. I moved closer to him and took a good glance at his left cheek. Then I put the fingertips of my right hand on it and gently ran them down his cheek.

"You have a scar that I didn't see on you in Paris."

"It was throbbing badly when it first happened."

"It looks sore. How did it happen?"

"I got knifed inside the Métro station."

"At night?"

"At night!"

"Why were you there?"

"Trying to find a place to sleep. The spot where you and I — and Aubrey — stayed the night is my usual hideout. But... After you left, I was unable to go back there. I would've been haunted by memories of you and our last hours together." I nodded at his revelation. "Now I tend to roam Paris for a new spot. Sometimes I come across people who... have no good intentions."

"What about the hotel Aubrey and I stayed at? They wouldn't have a spot for you to sleep?"

"They wouldn't let me stay for free."

"How did you end up with this life outdoors in a metropolitan like Paris?"

"I was married. My wife died in childbirth. So did our baby, a girl. — I lost my footing in the wake of that tragedy." Rudi dropped his chin and gazed at the folded hands in his lap. I felt empathy but had no idea how to express a profound sadness on my part in regards to his fate. I lifted up his chin and looked into his eyes, my thumb still massaging his scar. A mere 'sorry' didn't seem to be the right word to say. Therefore, I remained silent, just mentally absorbing the moment of his disclosure. He moved forward, his face dangerously close to mine. His heartbeat began to reverberate in my being as I touched my lips to his, and we finally both surrendered to the magic of a real French kiss, long overdue. We stopped out of breath and slumped over into each other's arms, breathing hard. My breath slowed with my head on his left shoulder and both hands on his arms. It felt so good to be in Rudi's embrace. Minutes went by, and the two of us just stayed hovering in the present moment. I wasted no thought on the past and none on the future.

"Does he know I am staying at your house?" Rudi sounded on guard.

"Who? My dad?" My voice sounded hoarse from a dry throat.

"This guy! Your boyfriend... Gert, or whatever his name is." I detached from Rudi and sat down on the attic bed with the taupe-coloured sheets that I liked a great deal.

"Now you are spoiling the moment, Rudi! To answer your question, yes, I told him about you."

"Did you tell him that I am staying at your house?"

"I did."

"What did he say?"

"Nothing!"

"He was indifferent?"

"I am not sure. He didn't make any comments."

"Not jealous?"

"I didn't probe him."

"You didn't sense any jealousy?"

"Rudi! I didn't pay that much attention to his nonverbal communication."

"Carielle, did he not want to come up to spend the night... With you?" I smirked at Rudi's bluntness.

"He might have wanted to but... My parents won't have it." It took Rudi a moment to absorb what I had said. Then we both burst out into subdued laughter with tears of amusement beginning to roll from our eyes.

***

The next morning, Rudi made an appearance in my mom's kitchen and sat down at the table like a member of the family. It was the time zone between breakfast and lunch. Nothing was served. I knew how reluctant my mother felt about meeting Rudi. She stayed away for about ten minutes. I was beginning to feel embarrassed.

"Can I offer you anything at all, Rudi? A bowl of cornflakes, coffee, a piece of cheesecake, tea, or... toast?"

"A cup of strong coffee, please, and a piece of German cheesecake would make my day." From his sitting position, he looked up at me with that irresistible smile. I returned his grin, and right then my mother entered the kitchen. Rudi stood up.

"Good morning, Rudi. Nice to meet you!" My mom shook his hand and turned away as soon as the words were out.

"Pleased to meet you as well, Mrs. Sander!" Rudi looked embarrassed and unsure about how to continue.

"I hope you're enjoying your stay upstairs." My mother fleetingly said it, distracted and uninterested.

"Mom, Rudi will be leaving tomorrow. Would I be able to borrow your car to drive him... to...?" I didn't finish the question because Rudi hadn't told me where he wanted me to drop him off.

"Ask me again later!" My mother sounded rude, and her answer left no room for debate.

"Alright then!" My response was just loud enough to be heard, and to my dismay, Rudi was about to pull a pack of Gauloises from his shirt pocket. I tried to send him a signal of disapproval, but he didn't see it. Before I could get his attention, he lit up, in the middle of my mom's treasured kitchen. I could sense that my mother would've liked to tell him off and kick him out. I also knew I would eventually hear about it. Clearly, the morning wasn't going well.

***

I cancelled my date with Gert, giving next to no reason why. The phone call took less than three minutes. I would deal with Gert the next day, or the day after. Again, Rudi and I were sitting cross-legged upstairs in the attic, facing each other...

"Would you like to go sightseeing? We could walk or take the city train downtown." I felt guilty about not having enough to offer.

"I've come to spend time with you. City life is the same everywhere. No need to roam the streets of Brunswick. I do enough of that in Paris. Come here!" I sat down beside him on the bed's mattress but did not look at him.

"Nap time," I jokingly said under my breath and curled up on my side on top of the taupe duvet. Rudi moved to lie down beside me with his chest against my back and his abdomen against my *derrière*. He put his right arm around me and rested his hand on my stomach. I turned my head somewhat, trying to face him, one reason being I wanted to tune out the pleasurable sensation his closeness gave me.

"Hey, Rudi, what did you do for a living before you started your life as a *clochard*?" I felt the urgent need to know more after all this time of tapping in the dark.

"Random jobs, some for the Moroccans."

"Your response is as vague as ever, other than the mention of the Moroccans. Do they all live in that particular hotel that you took us to?"

"Some, and others nearby." Rudi, still relaxed a moment ago, clearly began to feel apprehensive. I could feel his muscles tense, and he slightly moved away from me.

"What is it? Why are you moving away from me?" He instantly snuggled up again, far away from the present moment, as it felt.

"My closeness should make you feel boiling hot on the inside," Rudi said, grinning. He lifted himself up and rolled me onto my back. In an instant, he was on top of me, his smiling eyes meeting mine. "Just a word of caution, Carielle! Be wise not to travel to metropolitans like Paris on your own or with a girlfriend." I perked up. Then I frowned right into his face. "A lot of beautiful women have disappeared in Paris, never to be seen again." Rudi looked concerned.

"Why? How would you know?" I stammered.

"The likes of you get sold for an exorbitant amount and shipped to the Middle East to work in harems. Period." Now it was my turn to tense under Rudi's weight.

"You could've sold me? Is that what you meant to say?"

"I could've." He scanned my face, likely waiting for a potentially heated response.

"Why didn't you?" It was the only reply I could think of. I felt calm like the surface of the sea on random days.

"When they asked me how much I wanted for you, I said no."

"And... They accepted your refusal just like that?" The story around my potential sale in Paris was getting more intriguing by the second.

"They accept it when I have a good enough reason. I wanted you for myself."

"For business?"

"Potential business and personal!"

"Do you want me to believe all of this?"

"You may, or you may not. It's up to you. The bottom line is that the real reason for my choice had nothing to do with business or personal gains."

"Tell me the reason," I whispered in his ear when his contemplation took too long.

"I needed to protect you, regardless of my own personal interest."

"What? You needed to protect me without getting anything out of it for yourself?"

"Precisely!"

"I don't understand."

"Neither do I."

"Let's say you would've sold me. What would've happened to Aubrey?" Rudi sighed audibly.

"Obese Aubrey..." Rudi laughed out loud. Then he murmured in his quietest voice. "She would've been killed and tossed into the Seine." On that note, I held my breath; my mouth dropped open. No sound came out.

"I'll give you time to digest it," he offered generously, then was about to sit up.

"Stay with me!" I sounded soft like a gentle wave of caressing air.

"I'd gladly stay and move in a little closer," Rudi volunteered. I ignored his provocation.

"Is this why you tensed up when I asked about your... way of... making... money? With the Moroccans?"

"The Moroccans, East Indians, and others."

"Rudi, you are a criminal!" I was stunned about this ongoing revelation.

"It looks like it, but I am not actively involved. Plus, you asked. There's your answer, and your curiosity should be satisfied now."

"Not actively involved? Is there something like passively involved?"

"I get paid for hints. You were the only one in a long time who I could've handed over, but, you see, I didn't. I am not all bad." I froze.

"Were you thinking about selling me when you met me at the youth hostel?"

"Somewhat!"

"You are leading a dangerous life, Rudi." He looked sad all of a sudden and touched the scar on his cheek.

"I'll be dead next!"

"Don't say that, please! We all have good and bad traits. One trait is always more pronounced than the other, and it changes — like the yin yang."

"And?"

"I have a crush on you." The words tumbled out of my mouth before I could think twice.

"That's because I have an unusual life that you find attractive." He turned serious as he carried on. "Carielle, this is our chance. I'll be leaving tomorrow." His eyes met mine with enormous intensity. He kissed my forehead, my nose, and then his lips found my mouth for another taste of an ardent kiss with tongues, light at first, then increasing in potency. We didn't take the time to catch our breaths. Our French kissing went on undisturbed in — what seemed like — a state where space and time did not exist. Rudi stopped for a moment only to make me aware of something. "You've been putting this off. You've wanted it all along." I refrained from responding as he continued inundating me with kisses and caresses. My resistance to love-making had finally worn off, and I allowed his approach to happen and take me over. His soft touch ignited my skin and my senses and propelled forward my sexual response. Shirts and jeans were stripped and urgently tossed through the air across the attic. My shirt landed on the window crank handle and swung back and forth. We laughed and laughed. Then magic was happening unhurriedly up to a fleeting moment of blissful delight... —

***

Though nineteen years old, I had difficulty facing my mother the next day and looking her in the eyes. It felt like I had done something forbidden in my parents' house. My dad was absent as on most days, and he likely chose to be oblivious. My mother had a keener sense of what was going on around her daughters.

I sat down at the breakfast table, wishing I was in Paris where no parental eye would be able to watch my every step. In Paris, I felt independent and empowered. At home, I felt useless and small.

The piece of buttered honey toast that I had prepared for myself tasted like old chewing gum. I wasn't able to swallow. With every bite, I needed a sip of tea to wash it down. I kept staring at my plate, not turning left, or right, or ahead to the window that faced the backyard. Rudi had chosen to pack up his few belongings and freshen up for his departure. He didn't care to have breakfast.

"Mom, can I ask you again if I can borrow your car?" I put the question forward without looking up.

"Why?" Her response sharply pierced my sense of hearing.

"Rudi needs a ride to the highway exit west. I offered to take him." I waited, holding my breath. The pause seemed awfully long.

"No! You're not chauffeuring him in our car." Her reply sounded hostile and final. I stood up and left the kitchen without finishing my toast and tea. I left my dishes on the table, a one-time gesture that showed I had more important things on my mind than cleaning up. I ran upstairs and climbed the ladder to the attic. Rudi — sitting on the mattress with his small backpack shouldered — was ready to leave. I swallowed.

"I can't drive you."

"Oh! No worries! I'll..." Rudi acted surprised. Was he really?

"We'll take my bike." The idea cheered me up.

"Your bike? You mean... You'll be riding, I'll be walking?" He laughed.

"Not exactly! My bike has a fair-sized luggage rack that I can sit on if you want to ride the bike." Inspired, I waited for his input.

"It's an option, I guess. It'll get me there sooner or later. Okay then."

"Just give me a few minutes...!"

Eventually, we got so busy getting the bike ready and figuring out the shortest way to highway exit west that I failed to notice how I felt about Rudi leaving. Would I see him again? When and where? I was about to get ready for a short move away from home for my upcoming university studies. My life would be filled with new goals, new friends, new environments, new impressions. Would Rudi be forgotten?

"There! Tires all pumped up! Jump on!" Rudi instructed. I tried different ways of getting comfortable on the luggage rack. No position was in the least bit safe and secure. "Not good?" He sounded concerned.

"Not great, but I'll manage with my legs dangling down to one side. You'll have to go slow!"

"No choice on riding at snail speed." We left the patio behind the house, and Rudi started pedaling. It was an effort even for him. "This will give me the workout I need and haven't had in a while. Hold on to me!"

The ride with me on the luggage rack failed to proceed in a straight line and stretched out like chewing gum. We took breaks, and walked, and then tried again to advance on my two-wheeler. Often, I broke out in hopeless laughter while Rudi struggled on. After about two hours of the most unusual ride of my life, we finally arrived at the highway exit west. We got off the bike, and, other than cars zooming by down below at breakneck speed, our own silence enveloped us. We had reached the end of a short journey together, and we both knew it. The highway, almost sounding like a rushing stream, would carry him away from me to a mysterious life that I wasn't part of. We just now had to make an attempt at a final goodbye. Rudi slowly passed over the handlebars. Reluctantly, I took hold of my bike.

"It will take you no time to pedal home now," he said, sounding hoarse. I nodded. "Come to Paris! Your life isn't here." I shook my head. A tear rolled down my left cheek. "No need to cry, Carielle! We'll keep writing letters until..."

"Until?" I asked curiously, eager to hear.

"We can visit again, here or there." He pointed west.

"You'll hitchhike back to Paris?" I asked as if I was just becoming aware of it.

"Well, that's how I got here."

"I wondered."

"Now you know more than you should. And... That boyfriend of yours... He's not good for you! Break up, and move on."

"That's quite a statement to make while you haven't met him. Coming from you, though, I will give that advice some thought."

"You don't love him. You don't even like him."

"After yesterday with you I don't!"

"There you go! And one more thing, leave this place right away! It's not safe to be here. Bye now!" Rudi kissed both my cheeks *à la française* and turned to leave. He walked a few steps.

"Rudi?" I called after him. He turned around one last time. I waved to him. He waved back. Then he kept moving. I stood there with my two-wheeler leaning against my right hip. My gaze followed his every step down the slope to the highway. Then he was out of sight. I decided to put my bike down on the ground and walk a few steps, so I'd be able to watch him disappear all the way down the hill to the rushing traffic that was headed west. To my astonishment, and within the three seconds I wasn't able to follow his movement downslope, he was nowhere to be seen. I kept scanning the slope, knowing well that he wouldn't have reached the bottom in the blink of an eye. Not seeing him, I shuddered. Goosebumps popped up on my arms. Bewildered to the point of a light panic, I couldn't stop glaring down the hill. He was gone. He was really gone.

I picked my bike off the ground, jumped on, and cycled home with a veil of tears blurring my vision.

EPILOGUE

Paris was the most unusual trip of my life, mainly because of Rudi, who showed up out of nowhere to help us and watch over us. His life as a German in Paris was shrouded in mystery, and the hazy flair around him never cleared to the point of transparency. I was unsure about the little bit of information he shared in regards to his clandestine activities in Paris. While in this book I replied to him in an unassuming way, I did not respond to his revelation when I was nineteen years old. At that time, I listened to him in silence, nodded, and never voiced that I did not quite believe him, or knew what to make of it. At the end, he also mentioned casually that he might be moving to Argentina without giving specific reasons.

There was sexual tension between us. However, the intimate encounter at home, as described in this book, did not happen but maybe should've. We snuggled up to each other during our night outdoors in Paris.

Aubrey was somewhat of a rebound for a friend I had lost in previous years. We had no common interests and were therefore unlikely to be a good match while on leisure together. The Paris trip, however, was planned approximately six months before our graduation from high school. Our friendship took a hit at the time of school ending with my mother handing the bouquet of daisies meant for me to Aubrey. From then on, there were stronger hostile undercurrents between us, potentially noticed only by me. While the book brings them out, in real life, they could be felt but were never addressed. Aubrey and I got together once after the trip to exchange photos of Paris. Following that, I did not see Aubrey again.

My mother had not been a friend of mine in several years. She very much resented Rudi's stay, but, while not as rude as described in my account, she mostly stayed out of sight.

QUESTIONS FOR READERS AND BOOK CLUBS

1)

What is the difference between Carielle and Aubrey's personalities? How does that difference impact their friendship? What 'positives' and 'negatives' come to the surface during their travel together? Do they explore Paris with the same approach?

2)

How does Rudi come across as their leading light at the right hour in regards to saving the girls' trip? Are his motives completely unselfish? Does he ever reveal to Carielle who he really is? Do we get details about his life or just a general big picture?

3)

How does Carielle feel about herself during her stay in Paris in comparison to how she feels about herself while still living at her parents' house? What do her parents have to do with her view of herself while she is under their roof? How does that difference show?